CHRISTMAS CONFESSIONS

CHRISTMAS *Confessions*

KARA GORSKI

Second Chapter Press

Paperback ISBN: 979-8-9988763-2-5
E-Book ISBN: 979-8-9988763-3-2

Dedicated to front-door wreaths, sparkling ornaments, endless reruns of The Family Stone, *and holiday hearts everywhere—and to every woman brave enough to unwrap her truth and begin again.*

"Christmas isn't a season. It's a feeling."

– Edna Ferber

"Above all, be the heroine of your life."

– Nora Ephron

Seaside Secrets Beach Read Series

Welcome to Cape Henlopen—a vibrant small town on the Delaware shore where everyone knows one another, and no one knows quite everything.

The *Seaside Secrets Beach Read Series* follows exceptional women navigating friendship, family, love, and second chances, often while carrying truths they're not quite ready to reveal. While the books in this series share a setting—and several familiar faces—each story champions new heroines and stands on its own.

Start anywhere. Readers who love returning to the same town may enjoy reading the books in publication order for added depth, but every book is designed to be enjoyed independently.

Here, the next chapter is always waiting.

Other Books in the Series

Beach House Confessions

CHAPTER 1

The Proposal

December 16

LILA MONTGOMERY NEVER MEANT TO LIVE A DOUBLE LIFE; somehow it just happened.

She stands in the Salt & Hearth kitchen, pouring two glasses of Veuve Clicquot for Mr. and Mrs. Jenkins, who are celebrating their forty-fifth wedding anniversary, when Nate swoops up behind her, clutching her waist and sweetly inhaling the scent of her hair. Nate's culinary team and the bistro's waitstaff bounce to Michael Bublé's "White Christmas" as they prepare, plate, and serve. Nate sways, bringing Lila with him. Her shoulders soften. *Nate. He feels like home.*

All at once, he spins her into the restaurant freezer, nearly missing the Christmas tree decorated with kitchen utensils standing at the freezer's edge, and closes the door. He traces her neck with kisses and pauses at her ear. "I have something to ask you," he whispers.

Her heart races. "Okay." She tries to catch his gaze, but he traces the other side of her neck. "Ask me."

He stops, shaking his head. "Nope. Tonight!" He winks, kisses her once more on her lips, and disappears back into the rush of his kitchen.

Tonight! Her lips curve upward in anticipation. She brings the Jenkins champagne to Table 15, then makes her way through the cozy bistro to the foyer reception, ready to greet the last guests checking in, glowing with the persistent warmth of Christmas lights left on all night. After five years together—two in New York City and three on Cape Henlopen, working together to transform the crumbling beach house her grandmother left her into a chic coastal retreat called the Sandpiper House—Nate is going to propose.

By ten o'clock, all guests are settled with only a handful of patrons finishing desserts at Salt & Hearth. She slips up to the top-floor owner's suite that she shares with Nate. Bentley—their giant, gentle three-year-old Saint Bernard—greets her. She drops to her knees and Bentley nuzzles her face. "Good boy, Bentley." He noses in further when she kisses his head; it's their regular after dinner greeting. She stands up, still rubbing his head. "I missed you. You can come down in the morning. You know the rules—no dinner service."

She looks around the room at the life she and Nate have built together. Nervous anticipation returns.

I'm going to tell him the truth.

The truth has versions.

LILA'S BEGINS BEFORE NATE IN NEW YORK CITY, A WEEK after she and Tibby graduate from the College of William and

Mary in Southern Virginia. College roommates and unexpected best friends, they are ready to set the world on fire. They move their four suitcases into a four-hundred-square-foot studio apartment on Bleeker Street and purchase a vintage green velvet sleeper sofa along with a teak coffee table with a tiled top from Furnish Green on 24th Street. They don't have the space or the money for anything else. Lila dedicates herself to her interior design assistant job, studying textures, tones, and materials, meeting new clients and discovering new spaces. Tibby starts medical school at Columbia University, hoping to specialize in Obstetrics and Gynecology. They dream of *Sex and the City* lives.

But as the weeks turn into months, Tibby rarely comes home—medical school demands all her time. So, instead of sneaking in midday shopping trips, weekend lunches, and late-night bar encounters alongside her best friend, Lila spends most evenings alone on the couch, watching too much Bravo TV. After four months of too many *Real Housewives* and living too far *Below Deck*, she begins to spin her own juicy stories. She finds inspiration in her fresh, completely over the top New York City clients—some celebrities themselves, and almost all rising stars in their pursuits.

At the end of their second year in the city, Lila self-publishes her first novel, *A December to Remember*. Fearing she'll jeopardize her business relationships with the growing number of clients requesting her from Soho to the Upper East Side, she lands on the pen name Ellie Winter. And just like that, a hidden life takes root.

BENTLEY JUMPS AS THE SOFT POP OF A CHAMPAGNE BOTtle echoes through the owner's suite. Lila pours herself a glass, the bubbles rising as if cued by her own excitement. She slips into a lacy red thong and matching lingerie set that she purchased two years ago for this very moment and throws her regular PJs over them. She lights the antique cream fireplace that she and Nate refurbished to gas, its mantel laced with fresh evergreen. She connects her phone to the Sonos amp and puts on Tony Bennett's "The Good Life," cueing "How Sweet It Is to Be Loved by You" to play after.

Nate comes up an hour later, leaving the kitchen staff to the final clean-up and preparation for tomorrow's brunch. He pats Bentley lightly and goes straight to pouring them each a glass of Veuve Clicquot, beaming. "Let's sit."

She wants to mentally record every second of this moment. After five years of Nate's ambition driving their relationship, leaving Lila to subtly drop small hints about their next steps, never wanting to push, Nate is asking her to marry him!

Small talk fills the room. Nate questions changes to the menu of the annual Christmas Stroll Dinner—duck instead of prime rib, or in addition to?

"In addition to," she confirms.

He rattles off new celebrity RSVPs. "Meaghan Jones has confirmed for six." After surviving a Hollywood scandal this summer, Meaghan and her new boyfriend, Bradley Heartfield, a Cape local and owner of The Oyster House, have been in New York City as Meaghan tries on Broadway. But the holidays bring family together, so she and Bradley will be on Cape Henlopen with her best friend, Palmer Harding, and all their kids.

"Great. I assume with Bradley, Palmer, and the crew?"

"Yep."

"Well, that should liven things up at the Christmas Stroll!"

Underneath her calm exterior, Lila's impatience simmers. She tugs at the small strip of lace creeping up her behind and settles into the sofa, draining her glass. She's now a little tipsy and still without a proposal.

But, as if reading her mind, or perhaps simply her body language—do crossed legs and continual nodding scream, *Enough already?*—Nate kneels before her, taking her hand in his.

Every corner of her body pulses. The fire crackles behind them and through the speakers, Mariah Carey serenades them with "All I Want for Christmas Is You." Lila decides to overlook that this scene isn't as she's envisioned it hundreds of different times. There's no elegant New York City penthouse rooftop surrounded by views of the skyline at sunset, with a private chef and a string quartet. No intimate mountain getaway, where she wakes up to a room filled with flowers and a champagne breakfast proposal. No candlelit beach path leading her to a private dinner on the shores of their shared life. Instead, she's sitting on their leather couch in the owner's suite of the Sandpiper House.

Although the moment lacks the dreamy perfection she's imagined, the question will redefine everything. She will marry Nate.

He begins his monologue. They are the perfect pair—everyone says so. Nate's culinary brilliance attracts food bloggers from up and down the coast to dine at Salt & Hearth, and her eye for coastal elegance keeps rooms booked solid nearly year round. They move in synchronicity, finishing each other's sentences, anticipating the other's needs. They make sense. Their Instagram followers call them #relationshipgoals.

"Which is why, my dear Lila..." He kisses her hands. "I have something life-changing to ask you." She's drunk with happiness, and a touch of Veuve Clicquot, every inch of her body alive with anticipation.

"The Wellington Equity Group is offering me my own restaurant in Charleston. Will you come with me?" His eyes are bright with ambition. "You'll love the space. It's historic, brick walls, those beams you can't get enough of. We can design it together—your vision, my menu."

Not a proposal.

Lila stares at their entwined fingers. A weight settles on her heart.

"We've mastered this place," he says, gesturing around their perfectly curated living room. "The Sandpiper House has been a perfect stepping stone. But think what we can do with an even more impressive blank canvas."

She forces a smile as words fail her. Is that their magic? They build beautiful things together. Design perfect spaces. Create flawless experiences. Their relationship is an exquisite arrangement: She handles the aesthetics, he handles the flavors. They are complementary elements in a gorgeous tableau. Are they in love with each other? Or are they in love with the life they've created? A life that is only half the one she's truly living.

"It's the next logical step." He squeezes her hand. "We've proven we can create perfection here. Now we will do it again, somewhere bigger."

Perfection. The word echoes in her mind as she reaches for a fourth glass. Her silence radiates hesitation.

"I love you, Lila," he says finally, as if realizing his words could elicit the response he desires, his ambition tugging at her heart. "Imagine what we can build together in Charleston." His lips meet hers. Their kiss is deep and full and lovely. He takes the glass from her hand and sets it on the coffee table alongside his. He scoops her into his arms and carries her into the bedroom, where in a few short minutes he will discover her wedding proposal lingerie—business pitch lingerie?

Like so many times before, Lila skips the truth.

CHAPTER 2

Up in Smoke

December 17

TIBBY SNEAKS INTO THE ALLEY BEHIND RISE UP AND lights a cigarette. One smoke a day in the alleyway prior to her noon coffee settles her nerves, and has done so for the past eighteen months since moving from New York City to the Cape. It's her one concession to imperfection in an otherwise meticulously controlled life. She has to be quick and discreet because she can't risk anyone seeing her. She *is* a doctor, after all—and not just any doctor, she's Dr. Elizabeth Harlow—inhaling the one thing everyone knows will kill her. She certainly cannot smoke at home in the Sandpiper House's guest cottage for fear Lila will see, or worse, smell. Lila has a nose like a bloodhound and would completely go off the deep end.

Sure, they smoked in college, late nights at the Amber Ox Public House—everyone did, but Lila insisted that their William and Mary apartment was off limits. When they moved into their New York City studio years ago, they gave up the evening-out indulgence entirely. But when the mistake happened, long after Lila and Nate fled New York City for the coast, and her career began to quietly, secretly unravel, a cigarette and an extra jolt of caffeine became her daily prescription. She would grab a double shot of espresso from The Coffee Nook and sneak onto the hospital roof. While her residents prepared charts, she inhaled until her fingers stopped tapping. And that's how Tibby finds herself slinking into back alleyways before heading into the hospital to complete her morning rounds, reputation and accolades so far still intact.

She takes one last smooth draw on her cigarette; the tip burns red, yellow, and orange. She drops the butt, crushing it under her heel, and slips into Rise Up through the back door. At the counter she orders a cortado with an extra shot. She settles onto the high-top in the front window, sets down her Louis Vuitton, and begins to mentally review her patients' charts. Mrs. Donovan's test results, the Wilson twins' vaccinations, Mr. Grady's seasonal check-up. It's a practice that calms her mind and ensures no detail is missed, distinguishing her from other doctors as flawless. A mental exercise she skipped the night her world began to fracture.

"Hi, Doc Tibby!" A bright voice breaks her thoughts. Izzie, Chief Lawhorne's seventeen-year-old daughter, waves eagerly.

Tibby smiles, warmed by Izzie's energy and a feeling of home. "Hey, Izzie. Shouldn't you be in school?"

"We're in study hall. Seniors with privileges can leave campus during our break. So we usually grab coffees and a snack. Way better than the school cafeteria."

"No doubt," Tibby agrees. "How's your dad feeling?" Last summer, Chief Lawhorne retired from twenty years of a distinguished career keeping Cape Henlopen and Rehoboth Village safe and promptly suffered a small heart attack. He claims that being home with nothing to do is more stressful than any day on the force. The Chief has been under Tibby's watchful eye since.

"He's great. I mean, it is December, so there's plenty to occupy him. He and Mom are gearing up for the Christmas Eve Parade, spearheading the Police Department's 'Keeping the Coast Merry & Bright' float. Oh, and I'm working at Powdered Temptation's holiday market booth—you've got to pop by and try the peppermint Nutella crepe this year! It's like a Christmas bomb exploding in your mouth." Izzie brings two fingers to her lips in a chef's kiss gesture.

"I've had a few patients mention that Darby is pulling out all stops this Christmas season." Tibby's newfound respect for Darby Shaw surprises her. Since discovering her husband Jonathan's annual summer affair, Darby, town gossip and owner of Powdered Temptation, is transforming her entire life these days. She's lost twenty pounds, gotten blonde hair extensions and an extra-large boob job that has everyone talking. Even more surprising, she's kept Jonathan as her ride or die. There's no telling how she'll surprise everyone this season.

"Oh!" Izzie raises her finger. "Dad's also planning a spectacular New Year's cruise in the Caribbean for the whole family. We will be floating on a catamaran for two weeks through the British Virgin Islands." Izzie radiates a smile as if transformed into the sun herself.

"Wow! That trip sounds amazing! Sunshine heals. And it's exactly what this doctor prescribes." She winks. "Tell your mom and dad Merry Christmas from me. I will definitely see you at the holiday market for that crepe."

Izzie's enthusiasm for the season infects her.

"Merry Christmas!" Izzie backs into her group of friends and they head toward the front door. "Bye!" Izzie waves and then links arms with her friends as they all leave, heading up Main Street.

That's when she sees him. Through the frosted, snow-dusted windows of Rise Up, as she waves goodbye to Izzie.

Tibby freezes. Hayes Carter stands across the roundabout on Rehoboth Village's Main Street, his urban polish a striking contrast to the small coastal town.

She wonders if her eyes deceive her, but he's too recognizable. A tall, lean build. A small amount of scruff on his chin, but otherwise clean-cut. Dark, wavy hair that looks like he just ran his hand through it. His black cashmere peacoat. Holding his signature leather satchel and always carrying a notebook.

Memories flood back.

TIBBY SITS IN THE NEW YORK MEMORIAL HOSPITAL BOARDroom three weeks after a chaotic hospital shift. The president of the board introduces her, rolling through her accolades as if the twelve board members flanking her don't know. He lists her patient awards, published studies in the *American Journal of Obstetrics and Gynecology*, an elite roster of hospital donors all of whom she's personally wooed, and of course her chair on the board of New York's Worldwide Children's Foundation. She's sacrificed everything to be the best. Including a love life.

With her brilliance now on the record, she answers board members' questions succinctly. Within those walls, the board president repeats her actions back to her. Each one is justified, reasoned, and explained, if not somehow erased. She wonders if her ears deceive her? Her heart doesn't. They all rise. The doors open and they exit into the world, questionably unchanged.

The fluorescent hospital hallway lights flicker above her as Hayes shoves an unexpected recording device in her face. He's a journalist from the *New York Post.* He hurls questions at her like a circus knife thrower, with excruciating skill and precision, each one cutting her silently, deeply. Is she Dr. Elizabeth Harlow, one of the city's most in-demand OB-GYNs? What does she know about a high-profile patient who nearly died from a rare complication last week? Was a baby lost? Did a resident flag any warnings?

The board members surround her like bodyguards. She lowers her head, walks past, says nothing. Tibby's reputation stays intact. Her conscience does not. Six weeks later, she resigns.

THE BELL ABOVE RISE UP'S DOOR CHIMES, SNAPPING HER back to the present. Izzie's laughter is shut out as the door closes behind her, leaving the faint hum of holiday music playing from the speakers. Her eyes narrow as she stares through the window. Hayes Carter is on Cape Henlopen, standing across the street from her in the heart of Rehoboth Village—an unlikely coincidence. An icy shiver creeps down her spine.

What can he possibly want? He never published a story; the hospital ensured there wasn't one. But what does he know? What might he still be trying to find out? Her grip tightens around her empty coffee cup. He hasn't noticed her, despite her eyes glued to him, at least she hopes not. She can't risk running into him without knowing why he's here. The last thing she needs is someone resurrecting her mistake.

She takes a deep breath, steadying herself into acting normal, casual, suppressing the turmoil brewing inside her. She's eager to return to the sanctuary of her workday. The hospital is safe. There, she is still the unimpeachable Dr. Harlow—brilliant, efficient, and utterly in control. She's built a new life on the Cape filled with routine rounds, quiet nights at the Sandpiper's guesthouse, neighbors who love her and call her "Doc Tibby." If anyone finds out what happened that night at New York Memorial—even Lila, whom she's never told—her new life will vanish. *Poof.*

CHAPTER 3

The Guest

MAYBE.

It was the one word she could summon last night in response to Nate's non-proposal proposal, after getting tangled up in their sheets, when finishing off that fourth glass of Veuve seemed like a good idea. This afternoon, she drifts through the kitchen of the Sandpiper House with a lingering hangover and Bentley trailing behind her. She pauses for a peppermint-infused Nespresso, searching for anything that will calm her queasy stomach. The scent of mulled cider swirled with evergreen surrounds her—the inn's signature holiday fragrance, which she created by simmering homemade potpourri and tucking fresh pine branches discretely into garlands.

She refreshes her phone like a junkie. The *USA Today* Bestseller List will be published today and her fifth novel, *Naughty by Candlelight,* which launched eight weeks ago, has been on the rise. Since being discovered by book influencers,

Ellie Winter novels have spread across the internet like a secret among sisters—unstoppable and in everyone's feed. Women devour them. Influencers and readers anxiously await the first Tuesday in October, when Ellie Winter publishes a spicy new novel that has everyone reading.

This year's release has been her most successful yet, with readers posting videos of themselves curled up with the book by fireplaces, in bubble baths, and on snowy porches. Her boutique marketing team at Athena Creative, headed by the legendary Athena Fox, launched the #WinterHeatsUp Challenge ❄️🔥. Within days, TikTokers were showing how *they* turn up the heat this winter—whether a favorite spicy read, a cozy-but-naughty date night idea, or their dream casting for *Naughty by Candlelight*. TikToks with candles, slow-burn playlists, wintery flirtation, and even dramatic readings of favorite steamy lines from the book have sent readership skyrocketing.

Lila swipes her phone's lock screen every few seconds in eager anticipation. A photo of her and Nate sweetly kissing under the mistletoe, dressed in their ugliest Christmas sweaters, which they donned competitively last week at The Oyster House's annual holiday contest, gazes up at her. *He's right: perfection.*

Lila stares down at her phone. How can she not go to Charleston?

She surveys the kitchen, her gaze sweeping the room as Bentley sinks to the floor, succumbing to the weight of remaining upright. The marble countertops overflow with cranberries, oranges, rosemary, and carefully seasoned duck resting to room temperature. Wooden bowls brim with winter kales and pomegranate seeds. Nate and his sous chef, Tuck Malone, have prepped the Salt & Hearth kitchen for dinner. Lila's stomach groans so loudly, Bentley looks up at her. She picks up her mug and heads to the Hearth Room, still refreshing.

Please. Please. Please. Still nothing. Last week's bestseller list remains un-updated.

Lila sinks into a wingback chair by a roaring fire, which she assumes Nate started first thing this morning. Bentley plops in front of the hearth that crackles and casts a golden glow across the wide-planked oak hardwoods she and Nate refinished themselves. The windows begin to collect the first flurries of December snow. Her phone buzzes.

Good morning, babe. I'm heading to Charleston in two days to walk the space. Tuck can handle the bistro for a night. Come with me?

Her excitement dims.

Maybe.

Lila overflows with maybes.

Another buzz follows, but this time it's not Nate. Her fingers quiver as she swipes the notification open. A smile tugs at the corners of her mouth. She looks around to ensure she's alone in the den. Her feet bounce uncontrollably. "Yes!" She pumps her fists in the air. *Naughty by Candlelight* hit #8 on the best holiday romance reads category on *USA Today*'s Bestseller list, making it her second bestseller.

Within seconds, Athena slides into her DMs.

Eight is great! Next stop: #1 and done. 🖤 I know how to get there. Call u in a bit.

Athena Fox is Ellie Winter's best decision. Eight years earlier, in New York City, after a scandalous breakup with Little, Brown and Fox, Athena spun the fallout into her own empire, building a sleek, full-service book marketing agency in the heart of Soho. Lila was brought in to design the interior of Athena's new offices, from redrawing the entire layout to hand-selecting every finish and décor item, right as she finished the first draft of her second novel.

From the start, she adored Athena's brilliance and decisive energy; her quick decisions without second-guessing represented everything her other clients were not. Athena had an instinct for hits. So when Lila casually mentioned that a friend was writing a novel, Athena offered to read it. Athena's response was so effusive, so certain, it stripped away her last layer of pretense. In that moment, Lila knew two things for sure: Athena would keep her secret—from everyone at her own firm and beyond it—and she'd make Ellie Winter a success.

As the Hearth room fire melts to a simmering blaze before her, Lila emphasizes Athena's text with double exclamation points. A bittersweet rush of pride bubbles up. She wonders if the success of *Naughty by Candlelight* might trickle down to her other novels as her readership grows. She hopes that her first novel, *A December to Remember*—her personal favorite and, as is the case with many novelists, the story most closely based on her own life—might eventually find its way onto the bestseller list. She rereads Athena's message. *A top 10 Bestseller!* She wants to scream in celebration throughout the inn. She wants to run back into the kitchen, throw her arms around Nate, and celebrate with him. Instead, Lila stares down at her black phone screen. Deep in its darkened reflection, Ellie Winter stares back. Her nerves smother her excitement. No one walking into the

Sandpiper House would ever guess that its elegant co-owner and interior design queen moonlights as the author of seductive holiday romance books that make readers blush.

Her fingers hover over Tibby's contact, "🩺Doc Harlow." She types out a message and hits send before overthinking.

Naughty by Candlelight hit #8! 🎉

Three dots percolate within a bubble. They disappear. Maybe she's with a patient. They percolate once more.

😮 🥳 😍 We'll celebrate tonight! 🥂

Tension melts from her shoulders and she settles again into the wingback. She's not entirely alone in this secret world she's created—there's one other person besides Athena who knows.

Lila remembers the moment clearly. One early morning on Bleeker Street, Tibby arrived home from a hospital shift and discovered her sleeping on the couch, where she'd been all night. A working draft of her first novel spread across her chest. A black ink pen slipping from her fingers. A small trail of drool wetting her chin. Tibby picked up the draft and began reading. She was immediately drawn into the story; she couldn't put it down, reading every word rather than collapsing post-shift. Tibby's excitement ignited a bright energy within Lila, who swore her best friend to secrecy and never told another soul except Athena—not the guests, not the town, not even Nate.

Lila sighs, and the candle on the table next to her flickers. Everyone expects Lila Montgomery to be charming, stylish, appropriate; Ellie Winter unburdens all expectations. Would people take her seriously as Ellie Winter? What would Nate think of the woman who's shared his bed, his business, and his dreams for the past five years, all while hiding half of who she is?

If anyone finds out... instant mortification.

The bell dings at the reception desk, saving her from any more thoughts. Bentley opens one eye, rolls onto his side, stretches, and collapses back into his afternoon coma. Lila pivots into luxury host mode, standing and smoothing her blouse into place. As she approaches the reception, she spots a tall man with dark wavy hair and broad shoulders. Her gaze locks on him as she beelines through the foyer to the reception.

Sloan Price, a wash-ashore from Philadelphia who recently rolled into town and, like manna from heaven, volunteered to assist Lila during the holiday season at the inn, blurs her view. Sloan stands tall, clutching both sides of the famed Daily Board—a large chalkboard rendered in gorgeous hand-drawn, colorful details that announces the town's daily events and celebrations, along with guests' birthdays and anniversaries. At the top, Sloan updates a countdown that marks three days until the Sandpiper's annual Christmas Stroll Dinner. All at once, the floor taps with Sloan's stiletto knee-high boots, paired perfectly with a black leather mini skirt and a cranberry silk blouse, as she abandons the Daily Board and steps behind the reception desk. Sloan exudes attempted luxury. Lila has noticed that Sloan seems drawn to all things wealthy and privileged, which explains why she is completely transfixed by what's in front of her.

"Welcome to the Sandpiper House," Sloan gushes. Her Philly accent contrasts her opulent presentation.

"I've got it, Sloan. Thank you, dear." Lila dismisses Sloan, and her eyes meet his again. "Yes, welcome to the Sandpiper House. I'm Lila Montgomery." She extends her hand.

"Well hello, Lila Montgomery," he replies shaking her hand, "Hayes Carter." She's frozen by his gray-blue eyes, sharp cheekbones, and carved jawline. His skin is still sun-kissed from the summer. His broad shoulders elevate him to superhero status. When his hand touches hers, she shudders. He's exquisite.

"See something you like?" he asks.

Her cheeks burn red. *Caught!*

She snaps her hand back. "No, nothing." She shakes her head and battles a smile.

"Hmm." He winks.

Who winks?

He takes in his surroundings. "It's…quaint," he observes, glancing around with an arched brow.

"It's chic," she corrects him. "Don't worry—we have Wi-Fi and a wine list."

"Well, we can't live without Wi-Fi. Impossible." His white teeth shine at her in perfect alignment. "Sorry, I don't usually do this kind of thing. Inns, small coastal villages." He pulls out his platinum American Express, half-watching her, half-studying the surroundings.

"What do you usually do?"

"Usually…Saint Barts." His dimples meet her gaze. "I'm here for work."

She pictures him on a beach in Saint Barts with his top off and his swim trunks hugging his beefy thighs. *Heaven.* "What do you do?"

"I'm an investigative journalist for a lifestyle magazine. *Park & Fifth*?"

Her breath catches. New Yorkers read *Park & Fifth* right after they finish the *Post*—first news, then gossip. *Park & Fifth* is fresh, elevated, and full of New York's best secrets—the insider's guide book. "And what are you investigating all the way down here?"

He leans in close to her, "Something scandalous…or at least a few secrets."

She shifts away uncomfortably and notices that he notices.

"Kidding," he continues. "I'm doing a fluff piece on holiday coastal getaways."

Her antennae go way up, but she'll play along. "You've come to the perfect place, then. Come on, I'll show you to your room."

She leads Hayes up the stairs, the banister woven with red-berried garland and silver bows. "This house used to be my grandmother's," she shares lightly, glancing back as they reach the landing. "She lived on Cape Henlopen for twenty years after she retired. She spent her days drinking sun tea, playing cards, and making up stories about the neighbors. When she passed, she left it to me. Crumbling shingles and all."

Hayes lifts a brow, clearly intrigued. "And you turned it into…this?"

"With my boyfriend, Nate."

He lets out another "Hmm."

She eases into her rhythm. "Nate and I were living in New York." She raises her hand. "Former *Park & Fifth* readers. Guilty!"

"Love that," Hayes commends.

"Nate was a sous chef at 11 Park."

"Impressive."

"Yes, but the sous chef hazing at that place is beyond intense. Perfection is ingrained in his very essence—he refuses to settle for anything less, which is partly why he left and partly why we're so successful here. Anyway, I was stuck in a high-stress design job, working eighty-hour weeks for someone who thought constant yelling made designers work harder." She smiles faintly. "When the will came through, it felt like a sign."

"Most people would've sold this," he says. "Beachfront's worth a fortune."

"True," she concedes, stopping outside one of the eight oceanfront guest suites. "But I was burning out. The city felt like a box with no windows. I knew that on the Cape the windows are wide, often open, and their views breathtaking." Lila opens the door and steps aside. The sparkling blue ocean greets them through the glass wall of windows. Warm light bathes the room and bounces off the vaulted ceilings.

"Wow." He steps in. "Good for you. Most would not take that risk or work that hard." She senses genuine admiration. "Certainly not me."

"What do you mean? You're an investigative journalist, you work hard by definition."

"Some things come naturally. People want to talk to me." He runs a slow hand through his hair, showing off his strapping biceps, his voice smooth. He sets his duffle on the bed.

"When I asked Nate, he never hesitated. He said, 'Let's do it.'" Her own words hit her like a slap in the face. *He didn't say maybe.*

She turns on a bedside lamp. "We wanted to create a chic and inviting escape—for our guests and ourselves. I design the inn—every lamp, paint swatch, and book on the shelves. Nate designs the menus at Salt & Hearth—the attached bistro."

Hayes's eyes sparkle above her. She meets his gaze. "You may not spend much time in your room if you're so keen on uncovering those secrets."

His grin widens. Challenge accepted. "Oh, I'll uncover them, alright. I'm very good at my job. Look me up." He leans his body into hers and whispers. "I don't lie."

Lila straightens and heads out into the hallway through the open door. "I googled you five minutes ago when we were downstairs."

"Sneaky." His mouth arches. He leans against the door-frame, one arm above his head. "I'm impressive, right?"

He can't help himself. He exudes confidence. She fills with a hint of jealousy. "Enjoy your stay." She turns, heading down the hallway, head forward and waving goodbye behind her.

She senses his eyes on her back. Her whole body tingles with warmth.

"See you soon, Lila Montgomery!"

Hayes Carter—like the abrupt silence after the carols stop—is unexpected.

CHAPTER 4

Lies. Lies. Lies.

TIBBY SCOURS THE INTERNET DURING AN EXTREMELY PRO-ductive panic attack that evening. She searches every variation around *Hayes Carter journalist hospital scandal* and *OB-GYN coverup New York Memorial.* Only three links return, each one broken, leading nowhere. Her chest releases. She breathes again.

Next, she types *Hayes Carter.* Her screen lights up with pages of stories. His battle with the top brass at the *New York Post.* A leaked recording of a private meeting, during which he accuses them of accepting hush money to keep stories quiet. His firing days later. He doesn't go quietly. She clicks on the top one.

> *Award-winning investigative journalist, Hayes Carter, who was fired without warning after accusing his own newsroom of burying a scandalous story in return for a substantial bribe, threatens to take his own editors to court, vowing "they*

are complicit in a cover-up that goes all the way to the top" in a tense interview on News 5.

She flips back to her main search, scrolling deeper. Her stomach clenches when she finds Hayes's name attached to a draft story published to a Reddit thread last year. Commenters suggest lawyers stepped in.

She can't unread the thread. It's her story; close enough. He knows something went wrong. He knows the hospital silenced the *Post*, likely with a disguised payment, a detail she only now realizes herself. He knows there's something there and he lost an award-winning job as a result.

Reality settles in her gut. *He wants the truth. He wants vindication.*

A knock on the guest cottage door startles her—Lila's here to celebrate. She glances at the clock. It's nearly 9 p.m. By now, the guests are all checked in for the evening and Nate is still offering the last hour of dinner at Salt & Hearth. Tibby quickly navigates to Amazon and pulls up Ellie Winter's latest book page—a convenient cover. She slams her laptop shut, heart still hammering against her ribs. She scrambles to compose herself, smoothing her sweater and tucking stray hairs behind her ears, attempting presentable in lieu of cyber-stalker. She cranks up the speakers and quickly ducks to the back of the cottage, where she's celebration-ready. "Come in!"

The front door cracks slowly before swinging open hard, slamming against the wall. "Bentley!" Lila scolds. Taylor Swift's "Opalite" blares from the kitchen, where Lila discovers her popping open a crisp bottle of Veuve Clicquot.

Lila taps her on the shoulder. "You're not supposed to cook." She steals a brimming champagne flute from the table.

"This is the most confused charcuterie board I've ever witnessed," she says, her hand swirling above a large rectangular wooden cutting board splashed with cooked shrimp, quartered hard-boiled eggs, goat cheese, and signature red grapes. She grins ear to ear. "I love it."

"Some of us weren't born with your design talent," Tibby says, attempting to rearrange a sad clump of grapes. Their friendship was born over late-night ramen and microwave popcorn in a dorm room. "I wanted to do it. I want to celebrate you. And here you are dogging my efforts." She winks at Lila, who looks twice at her champagne before taking a first sip.

Lila adds some crackers, unable to help herself. "God, opposites do attract. I create beauty. You fix what's broken."

She picks up her flute, considering Lila's words. In New York, she broke everything, herself in the process, unable to fix any of it. She forces a smile and raises her glass. "To being naughty," she toasts. They both laugh; the release cures her for the moment. "Let's go."

She grabs the bottle of Veuve and Lila picks up her attempted charcuterie board. They settle onto the couch in the den, the fire popping softly beside them and Bentley sniffing the prosciutto that Lila dug from the refrigerator and placed next to the goat cheese with a drizzle of honey.

"So, do we think *Naughty by Candlelight* can go all the way to number one?" Tibby asks.

"Athena thinks so. I'm not sure." As Lila sips her champagne, her expression clouds. "There's something else I need to tell you."

Tibby's stomach drops. "What?"

"Nate got an offer. A big one." Lila stares into her glass. "A restaurant group in Charleston wants him to be their executive chef. Creative control, profit-sharing, the works. Last night he asked me to go with him. He wants us to open the restaurant together."

"Charleston?" The ground shifts beneath her. "That's... that's hours away."

"Six, to be exact." Lila sighs. "He's excited, Tibby. More excited than I've seen him in months. I can see the ambition stirring in him."

"And you?" She studies Lila's face. "What do you want? What did you tell him?"

"I told him maybe. Honestly, I don't know what I want." Lila shakes her head. "The Sandpiper has taken off; there's more to build here. And Ellie Winter is..." She trails off, gesturing vaguely. "Ellie Winter is Cape Henlopen. Her identity lives here. Shouldn't she?"

Tibby longs for a slow draw on a cigarette, the kind that buys her time to process. She recalls Lila's pros-and-cons list about whether to move to the Cape or stay in New York City—a list Nate's never seen. Ellie Winter sits squarely at the top of the pro column. Although people don't know who Ellie Winter is, they're pretty sure she resides on the Cape, a seed Lila planted in New York City to throw off Ellie's scent. She didn't realize it would eventually become true. But more than anything, Lila leaving would mean losing her best friend again, her confidante, her safety net. The thought makes her chest tighten.

"I almost told him about my novels last night. I thought he was finally proposing," Lila admits. "Instead, I received an invitation to upend my entire existence without a single promise of commitment to our relationship."

"Five years without a ring is an eternity," Tibby says, acknowledging the unspoken tension.

"And it was just when I thought we were getting to a place with the Sandpiper House where he'd see our relationship should have goals too. Charleston will be a whole next level of ambitious pursuit."

"Have you told him that?"

"Of course not. That would be…" Lila shakes her head, eyes locked on fire. "It would be too much. And now there's this other complication."

"What other complication?"

"Hayes Carter," Lila says. Tibby nearly chokes on her champagne. "He's staying at the inn."

She sets her glass down carefully, hoping Lila doesn't notice how her hand shakes. "Hayes Carter? The *New York Post* journalist?"

"Yes, the journalist. But he writes for *Park & Fifth*."

Now. Now he writes for Park & Fifth.

"He's infuriating. Arrogant, smug. But..." Lila hesitates.

"But what?" she prompts, her voice tight.

"He is ridiculously charming. And perceptive. It's like he actually sees you." Lila looks up, her expression troubled.

The room shrinks around Tibby. She stands abruptly, needing to move, needing space. "And you think he's here because...?"

"He says he's doing a story on coastal holiday getaways. He seems genuinely interested in everything about Cape Henlopen—the people, the businesses, the hospital."

The hospital. She adds wood to the fire, buying herself precious seconds to regain her composure.

"You should have seen him at dinner," Lila continues. "Charming Mrs. Abernathy into telling him all about the town's history."

"Sounds like you're paying close attention to Mr. Carter."

Lila's cheeks go red. "Well, Athena says that *Modern Muse* wants Ellie Winter on camera. Apparently, they are running a 12 Days of Inspiration holiday digital series, and they approached the agency about an Ellie Winter exclusive in-person interview."

Exhilaration replaces Tibby's anxiety. *Modern Muse* entices women with the *Vogue*-like polish of their quarterly prints combined with the Oprah-esque emotional draw of their online media presence.

"Li, this is fabulous!" she gushes. "They are *crème de la crème*."

"Athena thinks that if I do the interview, *Naughty by Candlelight* will go to number one, and sales of my other books will skyrocket, even though Christmas technically will be over. They want Ellie Winter to be the final interview in the series, dropping into women's inboxes and the *Modern Muse* YouTube channel on Christmas Day. They are calling it #unwrapyourtruth." Lila slips from the couch onto the floor and buries her face in Bentley's fur. "I can't do it."

"Why not?" she asks, her voice gentler now. She turns, fire poker still in hand. "You've worked so hard for this, Li. You deserve the recognition."

"Because Nate doesn't even know. My parents don't know. Nobody knows except you and Athena." She smooths Bentley's fur and he rolls onto his back, politely asking for more. "What if they think it's ridiculous? What if they think *I'm* ridiculous? You know how mortified my mother would be—after all this time spent perfectly concealing her quirky, artistic daughter, who now reveals herself as a risqué romance writer? She'd be polishing her crown of disapproval and I'd be wallowing in humiliation."

"She doesn't deserve a crown," Tibby admits.

"Ellie is brazen and seductive—things I'm not. It's hard for *me* to reconcile who I am professionally with Ellie's boldness. How will others be able to? I mean, what about you? Dr. Elizabeth Harlow, New York's premier baby doctor sought out by celebrities and high society, has a best friend who writes smutty Christmas novels. How would that sound to you?"

Her face hardens slightly. "Don't do that. Don't diminish yourself because you think someone else's work is somehow more important, more valid." She sets down her glass. "Trust me, impressive careers aren't always what they seem."

"What does that mean?" Lila asks. "What's going on with you?"

"Nothing," Tibby says quickly, waving her hand through the air. She leans the poker against the white brick fireplace. She collapses onto the floor at the other side of Bentley, rubbing the fur on his nose. "You should be proud of what you've built. Your books bring people joy. That matters."

Lila shakes her head. "And now Hayes shows up here today. It's too much of a coincidence. I think someone's trying to out me." Lila looks away. "I can't bring myself to tell Nate. Ellie Winter is my superpower; under her cover I can be fully myself. She frees me from being paralyzed by everyone else's expectations. I don't worry about what my mother thinks, or fear jeopardizing my reputation as a sophisticated designer with my clients, or risk that Nate might not even recognize me. So, if Hayes is here to expose me…" Lila can't finish.

"We don't know that's why he's here," she reaches for Lila's hand. "Whatever happens, I've got your back. Always have."

Bentley rises, shakes himself off, and curls up once more alongside the couch. She leans back against the couch, still sitting on the floor and staring into the fire.

"I know," Lila sits beside her and lays her head on Tibby's shoulder. "That's why you're the only one I trust with all my secrets."

She grabs a blanket from the couch, wrapping herself and Lila together, enveloping them in a warm cocoon. "Right. No secrets between us."

CHAPTER 5

Coastal Confidential

December 18

NATE HOLDS LILA'S HAND AS THEY WALK UP THE SNOW-dusted walkway to the stately white colonial with a sweeping porch, its railing garlanded with fragrant pine. Twin porch swings, embellished with navy and red plaid pillows, flank the entrance. He knocks on the black, oversized front door adorned with a large eucalyptus and evergreen wreath. As they wait, he wraps her in a tender embrace and sweetly kisses her beneath the mistletoe suspended from the chandelier above. Her shoulders release.

The door swings open with a jingle. "Welcome to *Coastal Confidential: Sleigh the Season Edition*," says a tall blonde woman in a green dress and black boots, sleigh bells trimming her neck. She oozes with seasonal cheer.

"Ivy!" Lila breaks from Nate and embraces her. "You look *so* ready to slay this podcast." She enters the foyer.

"Dress for success! Isn't that what they say?" Ivy Blake's southern drawl seduces listeners who tune in weekly as Ivy spills all the salty tea on Cape Henlopen and beyond. Ivy dishes on everything from seaside scandals—the mysterious "For Sale" sign on the boardwalk or a fallout from the local charity gala—and town traditions to the movers, shakers, and secret heartbreakers of the Delaware coast. She features interviews with beloved locals, anonymous call-ins, and the occasional cameo from out-of-town celebrities. *Coastal Confidential* is part news, part nostalgia, and all drama. Lila is not immune.

"Ms. Blake," Nate kisses her cheek and hands her a still warm panettone from Salt & Hearth wrapped neatly in butcher paper and tied with a black velvet bow. "For you," he says with a bow, addressing Ivy as the queen she is. Since opening the Sandpiper House, Nate and Lila gift local friends and businesses with Nate's signature panettone—grand chocolate, Sorrento lemon, or amaretto—every holiday season. Nate prepares one batch only, making the panettone highly coveted.

"Oh my, y'all. This trades for gold around here. And possibly Bitcoin!" Ivy says taking the panettone. "Mine better be grand chocolate!" Nate and Lila slip off their winter coats, hanging them on the corner coat tree, which boasts a red bow at its crown. "Come on, let's set this in the kitchen, grab coffees, and head down to the studio. Barry's setting everything up." Barry Barnes, a long-time local radio producer, provides the technical mastermind behind *Coastal Confidential.* Some in town speculate he may share a bed with Ivy—although that's the one rumor Ivy keeps under the covers.

Three steaming cappuccinos later, she finds herself seated between Nate and Ivy in Ivy's basement podcast studio that boasts no windows, plush carpet, two upholstered sofas, a large round table, three seats, three mics, and a solid wood door. It's the quietest room Lila's ever sat in. The stillness should relax her, but sitting in Ivy's hot seat puts her on edge.

Barry gives a nod, the light by the door turns green, and Ivy begins. "Welcome, listeners, to *Coastal Confidential: Sleigh the Season Edition*! Pour yourself something warm and preferably spiked, because today we've got two of Cape Henlopen's most buzzed-about locals in the studio. One runs the hottest restaurant on the coast. The other? Well, she's the charming innkeeper-slash-lifestyle queen you all love. Together, they've been called the Chip and Joanna of the Delaware Shore because their golden touch is as undeniable as their love for each other. Our #relationshipgoals couple, Nate Caldwell and Lila Montgomery, are in studio to give us the skinny on the Christmas Stroll Dinner—do you have your reservations yet?"

Her cheeks flush. Nate's smile winks at her. "Welcome, you two lovebirds!"

"Thanks for having us," Nate chimes in.

"Always a treat to be with you, Ivy," Lila adds.

Ivy digs in. "If you're new to the shore, the Christmas Stroll is the Cape's most glittery, cutthroat tradition, with the Christmas Eve Parade a close second. Locals decorate Christmas trees all over town—businesses, porches…the bait shop! On December twentieth, we stroll, visit them all, then gather for dinner at the Sandpiper House, where we vote and the winner is announced by yours truly. It's part Hallmark, part *Hunger Games*, and Darby Shaw takes it way too seriously. The Stroll Dinner is a candlelit coastal feast featuring seasonal cocktails, local oysters, and Nate's boozy Christmas rum cake. Let's start with, are there any tickets left?"

"Ivy, we are sold out," Lila says. "Since the Sandpiper House began hosting the dinner a few years ago, it's become the most popular finish to the Christmas Stroll throughout Rehoboth Village and up the Cape! But…we always hold ten reservations for a lottery on December nineteenth."

Ivy leans into the mic. "Y'all, that's TO.MORR.OW."

Nate jumps in. "You can visit the Sandpiper House Instagram for a link to enter. You might even find my signature spiked cider recipe."

"Where's my phone!" Ivy blurts out. "Okay, Nate, any dinner reveals?"

"We wanted this year's dinner to feel magical. Cozy, intimate, and elevated. Think candlelight, fresh tunes, and a five-course menu—none of which you will be getting out of me today, Ms. Blake." Nate zips his mouth with his fingers.

"Lila, you've been known to incorporate a few surprises into your dinner decor. What should we be on the lookout for this year?"

"As Nate said, our phrase for this year's inspiration is 'fresh magic.' Think soft hues touched with evergreens, silvers, white lights, and, of course, a hint of the sea. And yes, we are always plotting a fun twist to surprise our fabulous guests."

"LOOOVVVE." Ivy draws out the word. "Now Nate, sugar, rumor has it there might be a few *famous* faces at the dinner? Care to give our listeners a holiday hint?"

"Well, I'm not saying Meaghan Jones will be there…but if you see Bradley Heartfield back at The Oyster House this week, you didn't hear it from me."

"After dodging an FBI arrest this year, I hear our former Hollywood sweetheart Ms. Jones may be up for a Tony! My

Christmas wish is for Ms. Jones to serenade us with her new Broadway hit at the Christmas Stroll Dinner!"

Nate leans in over his mic. "Wouldn't that be the icing! Honestly, we wanted this year to be over the top, completely beyond. This could be the last stroll dinner at the Sandpiper..."

Lila turns her head in Nate's direction with widened eyes. If looks could kill, Nate would be headed straight to the emergency room. She wonders if the Wellington Equity Group might be listening.

"...in its current form," he clarifies.

Ivy puts a hand on Nate's and slowly turns her head up to meet his gaze. "Pardon me, sweetie...please explain yourself."

Lila stiffens, her smile freezing in place. "Or it could not happen at all if someone keeps surprising the entire Cape on live audio," she interjects.

"It's pre-recorded," Nate justifies.

"It's still live. Ivy does not edit!" The words slip from her mouth.

"Ooooo. Can you feel that frost, y'all? Someone looks like she's about two seconds from throwing a yule log at her man's head."

Her eyes meet Nate's with daggers.

"Let's heat things back up with a quick chat about this month's beach club book selection, *Naughty by Candlelight* by Ellie Winter—a rising star on the spicy holiday romance scene, and as mysterious as a snowman in July. I just know everyone must be devouring this book in a single snowed-in weekend. Lila, you're a prominent member of the beach book club, but we know you've been busy with the Christmas Stroll Dinner. Any time to read *Naughty by Candlelight*?"

She swallows hard. "Actually, yes...I have read it." She hesitates, then decides to go all in. "I couldn't put it down, actually."

"Ditto! This book, y'all. I need a fan and a peppermint martini. A widow, a beefy lighthouse keeper, and a Christmas Eve very much not silent. It's sweet, it's steamy, and it has more twists and turns than a jar of ribbon candy."

Lila stares down at her mic. "Personally, I love the widow's backstory and her transformation from being extremely lost as a woman within society's demands of career and family, even before losing her husband, to really discovering her own personal empowerment. Even if that empowerment partially takes the form of a beefy lighthouse keeper." She looks up at Ivy, whose jaw is on the table. *Too much.*

"Ellie Winter has long been rumored to be a local. And I have my suspicions..."

Her stomach drops. "Oh don't be ridiculous, Ivy." She waves a hand through the air, launching into cover-up mode, intent to keep her double life preserved.

"Well, let's just say I'm working on a little research project of my own this Christmas!" Ivy remains on brand. "Nate, give us one hint about your signature cocktail for the Christmas Stroll Dinner," she commands.

He clears his throat. "Well, if your glass comes rimmed in crushed candy cane and tastes like a North Pole nightcap, you'll be sipping our Naughty Nog."

Ivy lets out a holler. "Whoa! Naughty Nog! That's right, ladies, *Naughty by Candlelight* won't be the only thing in town causing flushed cheeks and bold decisions."

Lila laughs a little too hard.

"That's it for today's *Coastal Confidential: Sleigh the Season Edition.* Join me tomorrow as we discuss the ornament exchange that ended a friendship, and ask what really happened at Darby Shaw's annual ornament swap? And, this just in…" Ivy's phone brightens with notifications. "We may have a fresh update on who Ellie Winter is! Until then, you know my rule: Keep your cocoa hot and your secrets hotter."

The studio corner light turns red. Headphones hit the table. "Wow! That was wonderful, you two. Keeping it spicy even in winter." Ivy stands up, and Barry motions her into his booth. "I've gotta deal with Barry. I'll see you at the Stroll Dinner if not before, meanwhile I'll be devouring your panettone. Such a sweet gift." Ivy vanishes.

Lila turns to stare at Nate. "What was that?"

"I thought I'd add a little excitement by teasing up our Charleston adventure."

"Nate, I said maybe. I did not say yes. I'm still thinking everything through. I need some time."

"Your maybes usually turn to yeses."

He's right. But she's not sure this time he should be. Each time she thinks about Charleston, dread grows deeper in the pit of her gut. She can't tell whether she's devastated by the non-proposal or if Charleston truly feels wrong.

"You should go to Charleston tomorrow without me," she says, punishing him. There's still so much to do for the Stroll Dinner. I need to be here." Nate's eyes droop dramatically, his lower lip juts out ever so slightly. He looks like a kicked puppy. The sight tugs at her heart, but beneath the pull her frustration over his little on-air announcement swirls. "Really, I wouldn't be able to concentrate." She backs into the door to the studio lobby.

"I'll FaceTime you? I'll show you how gorgeous the space is?" he acquiesces.

"Perfect." She responds instinctively. The words punch her gut when she hears them. *Too much perfect.*

"What's perfect?" A smooth baritone catches the door and holds it open—Hayes. His sculpted shoulders are outlined beneath his sport coat and T-shirt. He towers over her in perfectly scuffed boots, beaming a smug drawn smirk.

"What are you doing here?" she bites out. He's the last person she expected to see in Ivy Blake's podcast lobby.

"Ivy invited me," Hayes responds. "What's perfect? Besides quite obviously you, Lila Montgomery." She blooms as red as a poinsettia.

Nate steps forward and offers his hand, "Nate Caldwell. You are?"

"Nate, this is Hayes Carter. He's a guest at the Sandpiper House."

Nate's chest deflates. "Oh, just passing through, then. Pleasure to meet you."

Hayes holds a coffee in one hand, lifting it in a mock toast. "Quite the episode. I overheard the recording out here. Congratulations, sure to spike the ratings with that one." Lila glowers. But Hayes's steely gray-blue eyes meet hers like a hypnotic snake's, entrancing her for a single moment, melting her gaze.

Ivy swings the studio lobby door open. "Hayes, darlin', you ready?"

Lila snaps back. "What are you two up to?" *Are Hayes and Ivy teaming up to find out who is Ellie Winter?*

Ivy swats Lila's shoulder. "Hayes Carter, New York City celebrity journalist, on the Cape for the holiday season? He's joining me for my next segment, Lila."

"Are you always everywhere?" Lila asks.

"Always." Hayes arches an eyebrow. His smile makes her whole body radiate warmth.

"Let's go, Hayes!" Ivy commands. He pulls the studio door open for Ivy, who passes through still jingling as she walks.

He leans into her and whispers, "I told you. People want to talk to me. And I never turn down a good story."

Hayes disappears into the podcast studio.

"Wow," Nate says.

She and Nate stare at the closed door, equally captivated. Neither reaches for the other.

CHAPTER 6

Bad Decisions

December 19

TIBBY THREADS HER MERCEDES ALONG THE SHORE AND through the narrow streets of the Village, listening to her daily dose of *Coastal Confidential.* After Lila's afternoon with Ivy yesterday, she'd texted only one word in all caps, "DISASTER." Listening to the episode air this morning, Tibby shoots Lila one word back: "HARDLY." She understands why Nate pushes Lila for Charleston. He's constantly striving for success, and a next career move resonates. But Lila can't leave the Cape, not only because, selfishly, she needs her best friend at her side, but also simply because Ellie Winter belongs here.

She parks in front of Powdered Temptation, where her staff gathers inside for their annual holiday brunch, ears burning as Ivy welcomes Hayes to the show, and to the Cape, over her car speakers. Ivy prods, "You've written about politicians, power, and protests. Why a beach town holiday escape?"

Exactly. Why are you here, Hayes Carter?

"Because it matters. This story is simply a different version of what I write—the people, the traditions, they reveal who we truly are. Only the setting is different."

Tibby's eyes narrow with disbelief.

"You've been spotted in our library archives, Hayes. The word is out." Ivy digs deeper.

"Brushing up on town legend, Ivy. You know, I've often discovered that the best stories go back generations."

Her fingers twitch. She craves a cigarette. Instead, she powers off her Mercedes, personally canceling what's left of Ivy and Hayes.

Inside, Powdered Temptation resembles a Nancy Meyers movie set bathed in candied delight. The sugar-dusted creperie twinkles with garland. Bells in every shade of pink hang across doorways and counters. Miniature silver trees center every table. Pink and red ribbons turn pillars into candy canes. Tibby sits sipping a cranberry mimosa, a decent substitute for a cigarette, taking in the creperie and admiring another win on Darby's transformation streak. Her three staff nurses and two office managers encircle the table, debating this year's best holiday song—Cher's "DJ Play a Christmas Song" or Mariah Carey's classic "All I want for Christmas Is You." Tibby throws her support behind Cher, smiling and nodding, but she can't stop thinking about Lila.

Lila is suffering because of me.

Last night they huddled together on the guesthouse couch with Bentley at their feet as they devoured Nate's last two slices of chocolate peppermint cake, which he delivered heart in hand with a heaping side of apology for the *Coastal Confidential* mishap before quietly disappearing back to his kitchen. Lila detailed the two-page layout of the article she fears, envisioning every picture and describing each headline. Lila's words tortured her. If Lila understood the real reason Hayes showed up—to finish his story about the horrific consequences resulting from her mistake—the knowledge would spare her a world of misery.

SHE FLASHES BACK TO THAT NIGHT AT NEW YORK MEMORIAL. It's one of those shifts. A slow start that ignites into chaos. She's at the top of her field as a Chief Attending Physician at New York Memorial, the city's most elite hospital, on track to be the youngest OB-GYN division chair. She trades her personal life, highlighted by a two-year relationship with rising tech mogul Jack Whitaker, for a purpose fueled with ambition. Or is it ambition fueled with purpose? Does it matter? Her dedication is unrelenting, her faults zero.

That evening, the city is a blur of sirens and flashing lights. Black ice turns Broadway in Midtown into a slippery raceway causing a catastrophic pile-up. The emergency room pulses with screams and floods with people, when New York Senator Graham Delvy brings in his wife Margot. She's twelve weeks pregnant, and an airbag deployed across her midsection. Margot has only a few small scratches; complications aren't expected. A resident flags something strange on Margot's ultrasound, suggesting further tests. She waves the recommendation off—Margot's physical exam is good and they are too busy for indulgences. But within hours Margot's condition shifts. A rare placental issue unravels into a nightmare. Margot loses the baby and nearly her own life.

The hospital responds quickly; Senator Delvy is powerful and the press hungry. Legal steps in. The resident says nothing. The official report blurs the details. No blame is assigned. Senator Delvy's office sends a handwritten thank you note praising her grace under pressure and offering their extreme gratitude for saving Margot's life.

She keeps working. She shows up. She sees patients. She performs three deliveries and a C-section, all with meticulous care and excessive caution—each one excruciating. She barely trusts herself, her guilt constantly whispering doubt and screaming ineptitude in her ear. She leaves New York Memorial one night and never returns. No grand announcement, no farewell gathering. A resignation letter emailed to the hospital head, asking him not to contact her. She can't bring herself to tell Lila. Instead, when she breaks down in tears over the phone, she lies, telling her best friend a story she recognizes—that the stress and pressure of her career are breaking her. So, when Lila insists she move out to the Cape for a while, a place where they've spent many summer weeks together, Tibby welcomes the refuge.

THAT WAS EIGHTEEN MONTHS AGO. SHE NEVER IMAGined that Lila would suffer because of her secret. Lila suspects Hayes is on the Cape to out her as Ellie Winter in a sizzling exposé featured in *Park & Fifth*. The guilt bears down on her with such force that she tries anything to escape. Did Hayes recognize her? Did he even see her from across the street? Does he even know she's living on the Cape? Maybe not. Outing herself might be premature or, best case, completely unwarranted.

Tibby inhales deeply, setting her mimosa down as laughter erupts among her team. The front doors burst open in a flurry of snow-dusted coats lured by the smell of strong espresso. Meaghan Jones and Palmer Harding blow in with a gust of urban energy, arms overflowing with holiday shopping bags. Palmer beams with pink, chapped cheeks, her baby bump gently leading their way. She spots Tibby and immediately beelines towards her.

"Merry Christmas, Dr. Harlow!" Tibby stands and Palmer scoops her into a hug, followed next by Meaghan, who does the same. "Hey, everybody!" They exchange air kisses with everyone around the table.

"Merry Christmas, ladies. Join us, please." Tibby plasters on a smile and begins to scoot chairs together.

Palmer shoves off her coat and sits across from Tibby. "What did we miss?"

"We're deciding if Cher or Mariah deserves to reign this season."

"Classic debate." Palmer chuckles, but she doesn't take her eyes off Tibby. "You look tired," she says gently. "Is everything alright?"

"Palmer!" Meaghan reprimands her best friend, pulling off her oversized, unnecessary sunglasses and surveying the cafe like she's on set. "Well, this is quintessential Darby Shaw—too over the top and a little gaudy for my taste." Palmer rolls her eyes at Meaghan, who places her hand on Tibby's shoulder. "Palmer's right, you look like death."

Tibby gives a half-smile. "You two, such concern for me." They're right, of course. Palmer has been her patient, her friend through so much—from Palmer's breast cancer diagnosis to the joy of telling her she was pregnant, months after losing her husband to a sudden stroke earlier this year. Over the summer, a preeclampsia diagnosis threatened Palmer's pregnancy but improved under Tibby's care. She put Palmer on bedrest and personally visited her daily until her situation righted; she wasn't going to lose another baby.

Meaghan slides into the seat beside her. "May I?" she asks while pouring herself a mimosa. Meaghan's blonde locks cocoon her radiant blue eyes, which always sparkle with a slight hint of mischief. She takes a sip and waves her fingers at Darby.

"Are the kids back?" Tibby asks.

"Aiden and Bella are driving up from William and Mary this evening," Meaghan says. This fall, Meaghan's daughter Bella transferred colleges, leaving California behind for a fresh start on a new coast and to be only a few blocks from her new beau and Palmer's son, Aiden.

Nostalgia blossoms in Tibby's chest as the mention of William and Mary conjures a simpler time.

"Also, the correct answer to this debate is clearly Mariah—the forever queen of Christmas," Meaghan concludes.

Palmer laughs. "Quinn came up with me and is spending the afternoon with Bradley under the guise of helping at The Oyster House, but I think they're at the jewelry store."

"I've told him I'm not ready to get married," Meaghan attests. Less than six months ago, she divorced the biggest Hollywood producer currently in L.A. lock-up. "I need some alone time. I'm not ready to turn around and marry someone new."

"Technically, not new. Technically the love of your life for the past twenty years," Palmer says. "And how's that alone time going? You two live together in New York City and have launched a new restaurant on Cape May that the *Robb*

Report calls 'A Locavore Sanctuary.' One final note—divorcing Duncan Jones should earn you the humanitarian award at the Oscars."

"Details." Meaghan waves her hand through the air dismissively. Palmer rolls her eyes. "I want time to fully resuscitate my career. Broadway is phenomenal—challenging me to grow in new ways. But I'm still not getting the good roles I want after this summer's scandal. I've realized these past few months that instead of waiting around, I should create my own." She raises one eyebrow, nods with eyes sparkling as if telling mischief to please proceed, then slowly draws a sip of her mimosa.

Tibby looks curiously at Meaghan and then Palmer, who meets her gaze with wide eyes.

"You're trouble," Palmer says, glancing back to Meaghan.

"Always." Meaghan smiles, leaning back into her chair. "Oh! Speaking of trouble. Guess who I ran into downtown yesterday?"

Palmer tilts her head. "Who?"

"Hayes Carter." Meaghan pauses, savoring the name like a forbidden delicacy. "He stopped me on Main Street."

"Lucky you. Hayes Carter is built for bad decisions. That body!" Palmer blurts out. "Sorry, it's the hormones."

Tibby's heart skips a beat. "You know him?"

Meaghan nods. "From New York. Years ago he covered one of Duncan's premieres in the city," she explains, her fingers twirling a strand of blonde hair. "He lurked around, sniffing out the latest gossip, spilling on the girl who was Dunc's latest infatuation. So lovely. And now, he's here."

Palmer raises an eyebrow. "And on *Coastal Confidential.* Did you listen this morning?"

"Would not miss an episode," Tibby says.

"Ditto," Meaghan says. "Truth be told, I'm as eager as Hayes to find out who Ellie Winter really is; that's a story I can get behind breaking. I mean, she could be any one of us," her eyes scan Powdered Temptation. Tibby stares at the floor. "By the way, Nate was weird…right? What was all his talk about the last Christmas Stroll Dinner at the Sandpiper House? He tried to cover…but he's not a great actor."

Tibby is a vault when it comes to Lila. "I have no idea. Men!"

Meaghan's eyes lock onto Tibby's. Her head tilts. "He asked about you," she says as if remembering out of the blue.

"Who?"

"Hayes."

"Hayes Carter?" She hangs onto composure, her voice faltering slightly. "He asked about me?"

"Not directly," Meaghan replies, her gaze unwavering. "He was curious about a certain doctor who left New York suddenly for the Cape."

The words suffocate Tibby. Her mind races.

"I didn't think much of it," Meaghan continues, taking another sip. "But now, seeing your face..." The words send Tibby's thoughts spiraling.

"What do you mean?" Palmer asks, her curiosity piqued.

Meaghan leans in, whispering conspiratorially. "Maybe Hayes is here for more than a quaint holiday article for his lifestyle magazine. If I know Hayes, he's up to something."

"You've read too many scripts, Meaghan," she says.

"Seriously, such drama," Palmer chimes in.

"Excuse me for a moment. Too many mimosas. I'll be right back." Tibby fakes a bathroom break, disappearing into the back of the creperie. But instead of the ladies room, she slips through the back door and into the alley. She leans against the snowy dumpster, her shaking hands pulling a cigarette from her Louis Vuitton. She lights up and inhales, her shoulders slide down her back. She rolls the cigarette between her fingers, watching the end burn and holding on to anything she can.

CHAPTER 7

Surveillance

LILA MOVES THROUGH THE INN LIKE A WOMAN POSsessed. A clipboard tucked under one arm and handmade rosemary napkin rings in her hands. She's dressed in an emerald green sweater vest with a silky white blouse underneath and dark denim, her hair loosely slipping from its top knot. She navigates her terrain in stilettos as effortlessly as an F1 driver on the curvy, breezy Monaco track—with exacting precision and speed. The Christmas Stroll Dinner is tomorrow and she's barely staying afloat; all that's left to do is nearly drowning her.

Adding to Lila's massive to-do list, Athena calls this morning informing her that *Modern Muse*'s push for an interview now includes a deadline—December 23 with guaranteed publication to inboxes, YouTube, and social media channels at 12:01 a.m. on Christmas morning, a glamorous gift that will set mothers across the country squealing with joy right as they finish filling stockings and setting out presents from Santa.

"It's always been your call on whether or when to reveal Ellie Winter to the world," Athena says. "I work at your discretion on that. But should you do the *Modern Muse* interview, I predict the Ellie Winter revelation will not only keep current readers engaged reading all of Ellie's novels for many months, but also attract a whole new group of raving fans. Because, quite frankly, gossip glutton people today cannot close their eyes to entertainment news—they have to find out more. I think *Naughty by Candlelight* can hit number one by New Year's Day—a Christmas gift that keeps giving right into January. Who wouldn't want to start the new year as a number one bestseller?" Lila's heart races at the possibility, and her stilettos race right alongside. But still, she replies with her stock answer. *Maybe.*

With Nate in Charleston until this evening and the muddled predicament created by their latest *Coastal Confidential* episode, people won't stop calling to see if perhaps, pretty please, they can score a reservation for the *last* Christmas Stroll Dinner tomorrow. She considers that if all those people calling discover she's Ellie Winter they might stop, betrayed by her deceptive portrayal of herself as an elegant interior designer and host of the most magnificent event of the season when all along she's secretly writing spicy romance novels that make everyone in town hot under their skirts. *They'll think I'm too much.*

She sets the napkin rings on the back bar in the bistro for Sloan to finish placing them once the crisp white cloth napkins have been ironed and folded. Lila pulls out her phone and types out an announcement on the Sandpiper's Instagram page, with the names of the ten lottery winners to the Stroll Dinner, captioned "LAST RESERVATIONS GO TO..."

followed by their names. Hopefully, this will keep the phone from ringing all evening.

She crosses the foyer into the Hearth Room in search of the antiqued silver vintage votives stored there, vowing quietly to herself to keep Ellie Winter tucked neatly under the balsam-scented table arrangements until the Stroll Dinner concludes. Bentley trails behind her as if they're connected by a preschool friend rope, dutifully and happily following. She stops cold in her stilettos when she finds Hayes sitting in a club chair, feet up, fire crackling, quietly reading. Her body lights up with not simply nerves but excitement.

"More comfortable than the library archives?" She approaches and Bentley dashes ahead, sitting himself at Hayes's side.

"Hello, Bentley." He rubs Bentley's chest, then looks up. "The archives have their charm. But a warm fire and a highball of bourbon go better with this." He shows her the blue and gold paperback resting casually in his hands, thumb tucked between pages like he's been here a while. Ellie Winter's first novel, *A December to Remember*. "A bit more spice than I expected from a Cape Henlopen novelist."

She takes a step back. He's engaged in active surveillance. "You're not seriously reading that."

"I seriously am. Truth be told, it's my first holiday romance. Page 130...very spicy, very unexpected. Have you ever done that on a sleigh ride, Ms. Montgomery?"

She blushes, walking toward the built-in cabinets beside the fireplace. Her mind flashes to the scene she knows by heart on page 130...a guided sleigh ride gone awry, a snow drift, there's only one way to keep each other warm, a fire ignites. A scene not inspired by Bravo, but her own reality. Her first love affair in New York City. A carriage ride through Central Park. "How would I know what's on page 130?"

"How can anyone forget?" He smirks. "I'm halfway through this novel and I swear I've heard this story before. Even some of these lines sound…so familiar. Although Ellie Winter's version feels a little more reckless."

She avoids his gaze, "Well, I do read a lot of Ellie Winter." She bends over, tugging with both arms at the boxes of votives at the back of the cabinet wedged beneath garland strands. She senses Bentley returning to her side.

"For someone who runs a perfectly curated inn, you're a bit of a hoarder." Hayes stands beside her, peering into the cabinet.

She bumps her head on the ledge. "Go away, Hayes." She bristles.

"Can't. You definitely need a hand."

"I do not."

"Lila." His tone quiet and firm. "Nate is gone. You're holding things together, alone. Well, other than Sloan—a champagne chaser who clearly has other priorities. Let me help." He crouches beside her without waiting for permission and rolls up his sleeves. For a moment, they both kneel in front of the cabinet doors, fire blazing beside them, their lips so close she can feel his breath. He reaches in and slides the box of votives out like it weighs nothing.

"You're keeping first editions of *Southern Living* back here?" He grins, "Sentimental or just unwell?"

She battles a laugh. "They're vintage."

"They're clutter." He hands her the box. "I won't judge your aesthetic hoarding." She shakes her head. He reaches for the second crate without being asked, "You know, I'm really good at candlelight."

She arches a brow. "Are you Naughty by Candlelight?" she teases.

He rises, closing the cabinet door and standing so close she's drenched in his warmth. "Oh yes, I am very naughty by candlelight." Her heart jumps. The flesh between her thighs pulses.

The air between them sparks. Her pulse drums low, insistent, her body answering a question she refuses to ask aloud. He takes the boxes from her arms and she watches him carry both toward the main hall with Bentley trotting at his side like he's done it a hundred times. Something in her chest cracks open as she follows Hayes through the foyer and into the Salt & Hearth bistro, unwilling—unable—to let the distance between them widen. Her phone begins to play "Christmas Vacation," her favorite holiday ringtone, and an image of Nate, topless in his chef's hat, flashes on her screen. A mix of guilt and anticipation stops her cold.

"Excuse me," she says, stepping away from Hayes. "I need to take this."

Hayes nods, setting down the boxes of votives. "I'll start arranging these." She raises an eyebrow. Hayes Carter surprises again.

She answers with a quick swipe, and Nate's face fills her screen. His excitement is palpable.

"Li! You're not going to believe this place." His voice echoes slightly, suggesting a large, empty space. The camera shifts wildly as he spins in a circle. "Look, I'm standing in what would be our dining room. It's stately and grand."

Our dining room. The words land like a heavy weight.

"Show me," she says, attempting enthusiasm.

The camera flips, revealing a sun-drenched space with exposed brick walls, massive arched windows, and weathered heart pine floors. Charleston's historic charm radiates from every corner.

"Look at these original beams," Nate gushes, panning upward to reveal vaulted ceilings. "And check this out..." He walks toward the windows. "That's King Street right there. Prime location."

She watches a horse-drawn carriage clop past on the cobblestone street outside. It's undeniably beautiful—the kind of setting that belongs in a magazine spread. *A magazine spread...* Modern Muse.

"What do you think?" Nate asks, flipping the camera back to his face. His eyes shine with an enthusiasm she hasn't seen in months.

"It's gorgeous," she admits. "Absolutely gorgeous, Nate."

"The Wellington guys are giving me complete creative control over the menu. Farm-to-table, but with a Lowcountry twist." He continues walking, showing her the massive kitchen space—at least three times the size of the Salt & Hearth kitchen, with brand-new fixtures. "They're even talking about a cookbook series as part of the deal package."

She watches Hayes carefully pulling the votives from their boxes, pretending not to listen but definitely catching every word.

"So impressive," she says, stepping further away and lowering her voice. "You deserve this, Nate."

"We deserve this," he corrects her. "This can be our next chapter, Li. I know it's a big change, but—"

A chapter without a proposal. She's spent years dropping little hints about their future, but now she's done. If he can't see what's right in front of him, she won't point it out again.

"Let's talk when you get back later tonight," she interrupts gently. "I need to finish setting up for the Stroll."

His smile falters slightly. "Yeah, of course. You're almost ready?"

"I was a little behind, but I have some unexpected help. Hayes is lending a hand."

Nate's face goes blank. "I'll be home in a few hours, Li. I can help with anything you need."

"It will be too late. I want to get it done. We'll be fine. See you tonight."

"I love you, Li," Nate says.

Will he love Ellie Winter?

"I love you too. Bye."

Nate hangs up. His words echo in her mind. *Our next chapter.* Her next chapter sits upstairs in the Sandpiper House owner's suite on her laptop—pages Nate has never read, a voice he's never heard. A wicked thought bleeds into her mind—if she never tells another soul, she could sacrifice Ellie to keep Nate. She shivers. Their next chapter feels like the end of her own story.

CHAPTER 8

Unexpected Arrivals

December 20

WHEN MR. GRADY'S SEASONAL CHECK-UP REVEALS PREVIously undiagnosed Type 2 diabetes, Tibby misses the Christmas Stroll. She invites Mr. Grady and his wife back to her office to discuss treatment options, ultimately agreeing to monitor diet and exercise changes for the next month before starting on any medications. She arrives late to the Sandpiper House, briefly popping into her guesthouse, where she lets down her beach-wavy blonde hair, applies enough makeup to hide the shadows under her eyes—evidence of another restless night worrying about Hayes—and slips into a simple black dress with gold heels.

When she arrives at the inn, the foyer overflows with guests waiting patiently in line to vote for their favorite decorated Christmas tree from across the Village. The Sandpiper's own entry—a fresh, magical themed creation adorned with hand-blown glass baubles in soft jewel tones, black velvet ribbon streamers, and pearl strands draped like garland—stands proudly in the center, glowing with warm white lights and gentle uplighting underneath. Brenda Lee has everyone "Rockin' Around the Christmas Tree" while they mingle after casting their Stroll ballots. She stands, momentarily transfixed by the beauty of the tree, the shining candles all around, and the festive greenery and florals that transform the entire space into a shimmering winter wonderland. Lila is a design genius.

She absorbs the holiday glow emanating from the room, watching the snow fall outside the eucalyptus-trimmed windows. A server passes an antiqued brass hammered tray of tall tumblers rimmed with crushed peppermint. Nate's Naughty Nog. She rushes to steal one, as if they are a limited production run, and sips.

"Doc Tibby!" Mrs. Jenkins waves from across the room. "Merry Christmas, dear!"

Tibby smiles and waves back, grateful for the normalcy of the exchange; the mistakes of New York feel distant.

"Dr. Harlow!" Sloan Price appears beside her wearing a cream-colored cashmere dress, complete with her signature stilettos and a strand of crystals and pearls that catch the tree lights. "You look absolutely divine. Your black dress is so chic—very Manhattan sophisticate." She air-kisses near Tibby's cheek. "Cape Henlopen is so lucky to have someone with your prestigious background practicing here."

She forces a smile, recognizing the fishing expedition. "Thank you, Sloan. You look lovely as well."

"This old thing?" Sloan waves dismissively, but her eyes gleam with satisfaction. "I was chatting with that handsome journalist earlier—Hayes Carter? He mentioned he's working on a piece about successful women who've made interesting career transitions."

Not a coastal holiday escape.

Sloan's smile doesn't quite reach her eyes. "Intriguing, don't you think?"

"Very." Tibby nods.

Sloan spots someone across the room with more gravitas who draws her attention. "Oh! There's Judge Morrison's wife. I've got to say hello."

She watches Sloan glide away, leaving Tibby unsettled but grateful for her exit.

"There you are," Lila appears at her side, turning heads in a bright ruby, pleated chiffon jumpsuit with a deep V-neck.

"Oh my. You're stunning." Tibby states the obvious and kisses her friend on the cheek.

"Obviously. And likewise, my dear. But you're late."

"Sorry. A patient."

"Speaking of your patients, Palmer and Meaghan arrived a few minutes ago. They're seated at table seven with Bradley and the kids."

"I'll head over," Tibby nods, scanning the room. "Any sign of our journalist friend?"

Lila's expression tightens. She nods in the direction of Scott Lawhorne and his wife Goldie. "Hayes seems to be schmoozing the Chief." Even though he's retired, no one can refer to Scott Lawhorne as anything other than the title he's earned with dedication and service for over twenty years.

"Now there's someone who knows where all the bodies are buried on the Cape," she smirks.

"Not all of them." Lila raises her eyebrows at Tibby. Tuck pokes his head out from the kitchen door and motions her over. "Gotta go."

"Good luck!" She squeezes Lila's hand and watches her disappear into the zealous crowd.

Tibby makes her way through the teeming foyer to the bistro, pausing to greet familiar faces. Salt & Hearth buzzes with excitement, glasses clinking as guests discuss their favorite trees from the stroll. As she approaches table seven, Palmer's laugh rings out above the noise. At eight months pregnant, she looks radiant in a flowing navy dress, her hands resting on her bump. Beside her, Meaghan sips champagne while Bradley regales Aiden, Quinn, and Bella with a story about construction workers flooding the bathrooms of his new restaurant renovation in Central Park. He gestures animatedly, almost jabbing a server offering Naughty Nog. Palmer gives an odd grimace—perhaps in response to the nearly toppled server? Tibby moves quicker in Palmer's direction because her natural reflex is to confirm Palmer's alright, but she's interrupted by a tap on her shoulder. She spins around and stumbles back on her gold heels.

"Jack?"

THE SANDPIPER HOUSE DISSOLVES. TIBBY IS TWENTY-SIX years old, swimming on the north shore when she meets Jack Whitaker. She's spending a week between summer med school sessions with Lila at her grandmother's house on the Cape. Jack is a sun-kissed golden boy who rescues her from a high surf that pulls her under, deep into its current. Jack sweeps Tibby off her feet the moment he sets her down on the warm sand of the beach. He's witty and charming, with a sculpted surfer's body. Their attraction is immediate and obvious, equal parts physical desire and genuine connection. She and Jack are kindred spirits, two determined souls chasing dreams across different coasts—hers in medical school in New York City and his in the tech world in Silicon Valley. After two years of bi-coastal dating, their relationship doesn't survive distance or their own ambitions. At least, that's what she tells him when she walks out and never calls him again.

AS SHE STANDS IN FRONT OF HIM NOW, THEIR ROMANCE feels like another lifetime.

Jack reaches out to steady her. "Tibby. How are you?"

"Jack, what are you doing here?" She takes in his familiar face, slightly older now with a speckled gray beard. His golden smile appears faded by life's circumstances.

"Callie and I are visiting my dad for the holidays." He glances at a back table where a tween girl swipes her phone, sitting beside her grandfather, who appears mesmerized by Ivy's polling of the crowd to see who received a panettone. "Since we lost Rebecca, I want to be sure Callie spends Christmas with family. My brother and sister, and their families, arrive in a couple days." He puts his hands in his pockets and rolls back on his heels. "To be honest, a big gathering distracts."

To be honest—the phrase ignites Tibby's deepest fears. Her gaze drifts to Jack's daughter, her heart lightly bruised by what might have been. "Of course."

She read the headlines about Rebecca Whitaker's car crash on the Pacific Coast Highway—*Tech Mogul's Wife Killed In Head-On Collision*—and sent the largest floral arrangement available at Atherton Blooms for the funeral, but never found the time to reach out. Or, that's what she convinced herself.

"Maybe we can catch up while I'm in town?" he asks. "I heard you left New York? You're on the Cape full time now?"

"You heard correctly."

His brows furrow. "Why? Why did you leave New York?" She's paralyzed by his directness. "I mean, you worked so hard for everything there."

She swallows her truth. "It became too much. I needed to slow down. Wanted to."

"Doesn't sound like the Tibby I knew." He laughs.

"Things change, I guess."

"Maybe." He arches an eyebrow in her direction. She could never hide from Jack. He'd see right through her to parts that not even she recognized, which is how she knew she couldn't stay after everything happened.

"Oh!" Palmer's voice, sharp with surprise, cuts through the rumbling chatter. "I think—oh God—"

Tibby turns to see Palmer gripping the edge of table seven, her face contorted in pain. Meaghan jumps up beside her, knocking over a water glass. The kids gather around them both.

"My water just broke," Palmer gasps, her eyes wide with panic.

Meaghan steps aside to reveal a puddle underneath Palmer. "Oh yes. It sure did," she says with inherent dramatic effect.

For a moment, the entire room freezes, but Tibby moves quickly, cutting through the crowd with practiced efficiency.

"Clear some space," she commands, her doctor's voice permitting no arguments. "Lila, I need towels and hot water. Bradley, help me get her comfortable. Palmer, let's see how you're doing."

Guests scramble back, giving her privacy. Palmer's sons, Aiden and Quinn, and Meaghan's daughter Bella create a circle around Palmer, who grips Meaghan's hand so tightly her knuckles turn white. From the corner of her eye, Tibby catches Sloan hovering near the edge of the crowd schmoozing Jonathan Shaw, as if they are both attending a concert—intently watching what unfolds before them and side-talking at once.

"It's too early," Palmer pants, fear etched across her face. "The baby's not due for two more weeks."

"You're going to be fine," she assures Palmer, checking Palmer's pulse and timing each contraction. "Both of you. I promise. We've been here before. Remember this summer? You're both going to be okay."

Nate corrals the dinner guests into the Hearth Room, where they huddle around the fireplace watching the flakes floating down like feathers outside the glass doors and windows. Lila races to gather supplies, her heart hammering. She returns with an armful of clean linens from the inn's storage as Bradley finishes transforming the scene, pushing tables back and creating a makeshift delivery area. Tibby kneels in front of Palmer, who now lies across several plush chairs pushed together, Meaghan supporting her head.

"The ambulance is on its way," Bradley announces, phone in hand. "But they're saying at least twenty minutes with the snow."

"We don't have twenty minutes," she says, her voice calm despite the urgency of her words. "This baby's coming fast. Your body knows exactly what it's doing." She smiles at Palmer.

"Like you said, been here before." Palmer bears down, breathing deeply as another contraction hits.

Lila kneels beside her, handing over the towels. Their eyes meet briefly, and in that moment, something takes over in her that she hasn't experienced since before the mistake—absolute certainty, unwavering confidence. Tibby is flying; the brilliant doctor she once was.

"I need you to stay with me," she tells Palmer. "Remember your breathing."

"Kids, let's give your mom some space," Meaghan instructs.

Bradley kisses Palmer on the forehead and escorts Aiden, Bella, and Quinn beyond the bistro doors. "Holler if you need us, we'll be pacing the hallway outside."

Palmer nods through tears, her face flushed with effort. "I can't do this without Miles," she whispers to Meaghan. "We should be delivering our baby together!" Tibby's mind flashes to Palmer breaking down in her office earlier this summer, still raw from losing her husband to a sudden stroke earlier that spring and convinced her breast cancer had returned. How wonderfully wrong Palmer had been. Instead, Tibby revealed that Miles had left Palmer with one last part of him—a part they are all about to meet.

"You're not alone," Meaghan insists, squeezing her hand. "We're all here. And I just know that Miles is here with us too. Wherever he is, I'm sure he's not missing the birth of his child."

Palmer sobs into Meaghan's chest, but Tibby pulls her back into focus. "You can do this, Palmer. You ready?"

"Ready," she whispers, nearly breathless.

The next few minutes blur together—she gives steady instructions; Palmer cries; the hushed murmurs of family and friends, unwilling to abandon such a moment, spill from the Hearth Room down the softly glowing corridor into the bistro.

The unmistakable cry of a newborn cuts through everything.

"It's a girl!" Tibby announces, her voice thick with emotion as she cradles the tiny, red-faced infant with a head full of curly black hair. "She looks perfect, Palmer."

All corners of the Sandpiper House erupt in cheers and applause as three paramedics barrel through the front door. Tibby swaddles the pink bundle in a kitchen towel and places her in Palmer's arms. Palmer reaches for her daughter, tears streaming.

"Hello, baby girl. We're going to call you Mila." She cradles Mila's small face in her hand and kisses her cheeks. "Your dad would eat you up," Palmer whispers.

Aiden and Quinn rush over to meet their baby sister. Meaghan holds Bella in her arms, both looking on at the completed Harding family. Tibby briefs the paramedics, who gather Palmer and the baby onto stretchers and into the ambulance. She walks with the stretcher, one hand on Palmer's leg, as they traverse the Sandpiper hallways into the foyer. She peers into the Hearth Room, where Stroll Dinner guests mingle while Nate reassembles the bistro. Jack is talking with Hayes, who leans on the piano holding a highball of bourbon. Her hands tremble, her momentary confidence evaporates.

"What an absolutely miraculous moment," Sloan appears at Tibby's elbow as the paramedics wheel Palmer out the front door. "You were incredible, Dr. Harlow. Like something right out of a medical drama." Tibby glances at Sloan sharply. "People would devour this all over the internet—the accomplished big city doctor saving the day in small-town Cape Henlopen. People love a good redemption story, don't they?"

Tibby's blood chills at the word *redemption*. "Only doing my job, Sloan."

"Of course," Sloan smiles sweetly and backs away into the crowd.

"Ladies and gentlemen," Nate's voice cuts through the chatter as he emerges from the kitchen alongside Lila. "The main course will be served momentarily in the bistro. In the meantime, please enjoy a round of champagne to celebrate Salt & Hearth's very first newborn!"

"I believe we've pulled off the most unforgettable Christmas Stroll Dinner in history!" Lila quips. A cheer goes up from the crowd.

Everyone filters back into the Salt & Hearth bistro, settling into their seats as dinner service begins, while Tibby gathers her things to follow Palmer to the hospital.

"That was remarkable work," Jack says, approaching her. "You haven't lost your touch."

His words sting like snowflakes pelting a frozen face. *If only you knew how much I lost—for us both.*

"Thank you," she manages, heart still racing from the delivery and his presence.

"I ran into that journalist—Hayes Carter. He asked me some interesting questions about New York." Jack's eyes search hers. "About why you might have left so suddenly."

"What did you tell him?" she asks, voice barely steady.

"Nothing. I told him the truth—we haven't spoken in years. But Tibby..." He lowers his voice. "What really happened at New York Memorial?"

"I have to go, Jack." She slides her arms into her coat and buttons up. "It was nice to see you. Merry Christmas." She heads out into the evening, leaving Jack standing alone watching her disappear, unanswered questions and unspoken truths swirling around him. Some things don't change.

CHAPTER 9

The Notebook

LILA STANDS AT THE SALT & HEARTH BAR WATCHING EVERY element of this evening execute exactly as she planned, exception to the gorgeous newborn baby intermission—and who could mind that glorious treat? The room glows with candlelight, casting a golden haze over dinner guests feasting on Nate's signature duck with cranberry reduction. Every detail perfectly fulfilled. A calm should be settling over her, but instead Charleston and *Modern Muse* have her unraveling.

Nate won't stop talking about Charleston, though he's barely talking to her at all. As servers clear the dinner plates, Nate moves through the kitchen doorway followed by Tuck, both carrying trays of boozy Christmas rum cakes alongside delicate Spode china bowls brimming with Chantilly cream, which are being served family style at each table. The crowd oohs and aahs over their favorite dessert of the year, some even offering a standing ovation as the intoxicating creation passes by before landing at their table. Through their accolades, she overhears Nate impressing Tuck with details of a potential cookware line, copper pots with silver trim and handles—"completely my creation," he tells Tuck.

Who else is Nate telling? Is he telling them she's going with him? He's been distant since returning from Charleston. When she asked if he was upset she didn't go, he said all the right things—that he understood, that the Stroll Dinner preparations took priority—but something is different between them.

He delivers a rum cake to Darby's table and catches Lila's gaze from across the room. She instinctively smiles, attempting to warm the chill in his stare. She loves Nate. Doesn't she? Even though he hasn't proposed after five years, despite their early discussions about marriage, despite her anniversary hints the past several years—she won't push. If he can't read the room, she'll make sure it looks fabulous until he does. Even though he's asking her to abandon everything they've built here for Charleston. Even though she's been hiding part of herself from him all along. None of it should matter. They're #relationshipgoals. The couple everyone envies. Perfection. How can she not love Nate?

"Alright, darlings—eyes up, glasses down!" Ivy's unmistakable voice rings out across the bistro as she taps her spoon against her champagne flute. "It's time to crown this year's Christmas Stroll champion—so if you've got any last-minute bribes there's a jar at the bar."

The bistro quiets. Across the room, Mrs. Abernathy lets out a delighted squeal. She pulls out a golden envelope from underneath her dessert plate. "I won!" She waves the envelope in the air, then opens it to reveal a complimentary Valentine's Day dinner for two. Lila's idea—a romantic touch to carry the season's magic into the new year.

"Well, well, it looks like Cupid's arrow has landed squarely on Bernadette Abernathy! Congratulations, sweetheart—you've just won the most coveted seat in town for Valentine's Day dinner," Ivy says.

"Congratulations, Mrs. Abernathy!" Lila shouts from the bar and raises her glass. She looks around for Nate, but her eyes find Hayes instead. He sits at a corner table, notebook open beside his plate, watching the room—observing with those gorgeous eyes. Does he see through her carefully constructed facade? When he catches her looking, he raises his wine glass in a silent toast, the corners of his mouth drawing that infuriating half-smile. Her cheeks flush with heat.

"Before I announce our Stroll winners," Ivy's eyes twinkle, "a round of applause for our fabulous hosts—Nate and Lila—for another unforgettable Stroll Dinner. That duck was almost as juicy as my podcast, Nate!"

The crowd laughs. Lila steps forward and Nate appears at her side, sliding his arm around her waist as he always does when people are watching. Together, they take a bow. She claps her hands together, acknowledging Nate, Tuck, and then the guests themselves.

"Now…" Ivy lifts a tiny silver envelope. "The moment we've all been waiting for. And yes, I triple-checked the votes, because Darby Shaw is persistent."

She unseals the card.

"This year's Best-in-Stroll goes to…" Ivy pauses dramatically, the crowd begins a drum roll on the tables. "The Lighthouse Museum! Their 'Christmas by the Bay' masterpiece features a functioning foghorn and delicately handmade papier-mâché osprey." The room erupts with cheers and whistling. Someone lets out an enthusiastic whoop from the back.

Lila holds a hint of disappointment underneath her gracious smile—a three-peat would've been nice.

"Second place," Ivy continues, eyes sweeping the room, "goes to the ever-stylish Sandpiper House because coastal elegance never goes out of season. Third place goes to our sugar-spun darlings at Powdered Temptation, for their frosted wonderland window display that actually gives you cavities." Ivy steps back, lifts her reading glasses to the top of her head, the pearled chain that grips them dangling down the back of her neck. Laughter and applause fill Salt & Hearth.

"Congrats, Li," Nate whispers in her ear. "You should have won." He smiles and kisses her cheek. It's the most of Nate she's had all day.

"Who doesn't love second place?" she whispers back.

"You don't?" he says with a laugh.

"I prefer first place, but I am gracious enough to allow others to hold the title." She laughs. "At least this year." Her phone vibrates in the pocket of her jumpsuit—"Christmas Vacation" muted for Stroll Dinner. She slips it out discreetly, expecting Tibby's update on Palmer and the baby, but finds Athena's SOS.

> Modern Muse has someone else if we can't commit. They want their 12th Day of Inspo to be an internet-busting reveal interview, pushed out on Christmas Day to inboxes and socials from their YouTube channel. All other interviews lead up to this last big one. We have to tell them by tomorrow afternoon. Call me ASAP.

Lila's worlds tilt, nearly colliding. An in-person interview with Ellie Winter to be put out on Christmas Day? Her fingers tap the back of her phone.

"You okay?" Nate asks, his breath warm against her ear. She wants to run upstairs to her suite with Nate and curl up with him on their couch, hiding from the world under his familiar arms that unknowingly shield her from her double life. He's been her refuge since her first affair in New York City went so poorly—a famous client she mistakenly fell for, only to discover he'd started dating another woman who would eventually become his wife. She spun her disastrous fling into Ellie Winter's first novel, *A December to Remember,* and dated no one else until she met Nate.

Nate is safe. But will he shield Ellie Winter in the same way?

"Fine," she lies, and slides her phone back into her pocket.

He leans in and kisses her, his iciness thawed. "Let's wrap up this evening," he says and heads off to pour coffee service, offer seconds on rum cake, and mingle.

Guests move into the foyer, gathering their coats, hats, and gloves as Dean Martin croons. Lila clears the last few empty dessert plates from a back table as Sloan primps against a snow-dusted bistro window, angling for the perfect selfie, her phone propped on a salt shaker.

"Lila, the Sandpiper tree looks like something out of *Town & Country*—you should have won first place! You have such an eye."

"Thanks, Sloan. I couldn't have pulled off tonight without your help." Sloan smiles, then gives her phone a sultry look as the flash goes off. Sloan wanders off, headfirst into her Instagram muttering hashtags under her breath—#CoastalChristmas, #SandpiperChic—when Lila notices Hayes's notebook. She looks around. No Hayes in sight. She can't resist. She opens the pages where he's left his pen inserted, raising it to her face. There's a single list titled "Cape Henlopen Secrets" with several bullets underneath. Two flash giant red warning lights at her.

- *Dr. Elizabeth Harlow – NYC Memorial incident*
- *Ellie Winter identity???*
    1. *Words Lila uses in casual conversation = phrases in Naughty by Candlelight pgs. 24, 89, 249*
    2. *Call Modern Muse editor previously at Post about Winter interview.*

Her stomach turns. She can feel her heart beating in her toes, her whole body is awake. At the very top corner of the page, Hayes scrolled in block letters the name "Margot," each letter individually filled in with crosshatches and underlined.

Who's Margot? She searches her mind for the name but returns a blank.

"Find anything interesting?" Hayes asks, standing behind her.

She snaps the notebook closed and turns around on a single heel. He stands arms crossed, his brazenly seductive grin penetrating every ounce of her. "I was...clearing the table. I didn't know whose this was." She holds up the notebook still clutched in her hand. "I opened it to see if I could get it to the right person."

His smile doesn't reach his eyes. "I'm thorough in my research, Lila. Always have been."

She spars. "Be careful, you don't want to make any mistakes."

He grabs the notebook. Their fingers brush and her entire body pulses. "I don't make mistakes." He walks toward the door, then turns around, "By the way, that Valentine's dinner surprise…like something right out of a novel."

Winter Kisses, page 75. Ellie Winter's third novel. *He knows!*

"I love a good series binge—Ellie Winter's novels certainly qualify. Have a good night, Lila Montgomery!" He waves the notebook in the air, his voice trailing off as he disappears into the sea of guests, heading out onto the wintry boardwalk. Hayes is crafting a story—a story that's hers to tell.

In the kitchen, she hears Nate talking excitedly with Tuck. Upstairs, the guests' rooms are full of people who trust they know exactly who she is.

She can't hide anymore. The time for maybes has run out.

Boozy Christmas Rum Cake

Cake

Ingredients

- ½ cup finely crushed
- pecans
- 1 tablespoon brown sugar
- 1 box Betty Crocker Super
- Moist yellow cake mix
- 1 3.5 oz box instant vanilla
- pudding
- 4 whole eggs at room
- temperature
- ½ cup Bacardi white rum
- ½ cup canola oil
- ½ cup cold water

Preheat oven to 325 degrees.

Grease and flour a Bundt pan. Do NOT skip the flour! Your cake will stick to the Bundt pan edges without the flour and the top will be ruined. Sigh. Sprinkle the crushed pecans over the bottom of the greased and floured pan. Then, sprinkle the brown sugar over the nuts. Your pan's ready!

Next, prepare the cake batter. In a stand mixer using the whisk attachment, combine the yellow cake mix, vanilla pudding mix, eggs, cold water, oil, and rum. Pour the batter into the pan over the pecans and sugar. Bake for 1 hour. Do not over-bake or your edges will stick to the pan!

When there are 15 minutes left for the cake to go, make the glaze. Using a saucepan with tall edges, melt the butter on low heat. Stir in the water and the sugar. Bring to a boil. Let boil for 4 to 5 minutes, whisking the mixture the entire time. Then, turn off the heat, remove from the stove, and pour in the rum, continuing to whisk until combined about one minute.

Remove the cake from the oven. Using a small fork, gently poke holes in the top for the glaze to soak through. Immediately drizzle one-third of the glaze over the cake. Allow it to sit for 5 minutes and cool.

Loosen the cake from its edges. Invert the cake onto a serving plate. Prick the entire surface gently with a fork. Slowly drizzle the remaining glaze all over the top of the cake, allowing it to drip down the sides. The glaze may pool at the bottom of the serving plate. If so, use a spoon to drizzle the run-off back onto the cake a few times. Some glaze will ultimately pool at the bottom. Cool to room temperature before serving to ensure the glaze has soaked in.

Glaze

Ingredients

- 12 tablespoons unsalted butter
- ¼ cup water
- 1 ¼ cup white sugar
- ¾ cup Bacardi white rum

Additional Notes

Perfectly served when the party runs late.
Known to loosen inhibitions and tongues.

CHAPTER 10

Fractures

December 21

TIBBY WRESTLES WITH A GIANT MAGNOLIA AND HOLLY wreath adorned with pine cones, dried oranges, and a burlap bow as she unlocks her clinic's front door early the next morning. She passes through the lobby, where colorfully lit garland hangs across the reception counters, illuminating her path like an airport runway. She stares at the floor for a second too long.

It would be so easy to take off, she's done it before. She could grab her keys and coat right now—no one is here to stop her. Her pulse quickens and her legs twitch with the urge to move in the opposite direction. But at the end of the hallway, a hand-drawn snowman, complete with a lopsided felt top hat doused in silver glitter and taped to her office door, catches her eye—a gift from one of her youngest patients. She stands straighter, walks into her office, and slips out of her long tweed coat.

She nestles behind her desk, flips on her computer, and grabs this morning's patients' charts. Laughter trickles down the hallway as the nurses begin to drift in. The smell of cinnamon coffee brewing in the percolator wafts around the corner. She inhales deeply, settling into her day.

"Good morning, miracle worker!" Nurse Evie shouts from the kitchenette.

Miracle worker! The hospital staff christened her with the nickname last night while Palmer and baby Mila settled in for observation. The delivery happened so fast. Palmer's water breaking. Chaos erupting around her as others panicked. Her calm, methodical experience kicking into gear, riding on pure adrenaline. Her steady hands delivering Mila safely into Palmer's arms. She'd returned to her old self in that moment, but this horrific nickname reminds her that she isn't the perfect physician everyone believes her to be.

"Good morning!" Tibby leans over her desk and shouts through the cracked door. She reviews each chart, closing the file and mentally reviewing the notes once more to make sure she's absorbed every detail. She oscillates between her files, her inbox, and her text messages. Hayes keeps interrupting her—sliding into the fast lane of her mind, surpassing all other thoughts to the very top. She should charge him a toll. Hayes asking Meaghan about her by name and her sudden departure from New York. Hayes telling Sloan about a different story he's pursuing, one that has to be hers. Hayes chatting up Jack last night in the Hearth Room—an old lover who holds a piece of her New York history. He's swirling. He's going to confront her. That's how journalists work, going straight to the epicenter of their story. That's how Hayes works. Her mind flashes with the image of him shoving a recording device in her face at New York Memorial.

The story has to stay buried. There's no proof.

She pushes her desk away and walks over to her wall that displays her greatest accomplishments. She removes four New York Memorial Hospital Clinical Excellence Awards. She takes down her most prized accomplishment, two New York Memorial Physician of the Year awards—given to one doctor across all practice areas who embodies professionalism, compassion, and leadership. If Hayes shows up at her clinic, he won't find any trace of her time in New York in her own office.

Evie begins to stream Spotify's Feel Good Holiday Mix through the office speakers. Sia's "Candy Cane Lane" lures Tibby back into her chair, feet tapping. She picks up her last chart to review and freezes when she sees the patient's name: *Whitaker, Jack Sr.* Jack's dad will be in at 10 a.m. for his annual physical before the year ends. His chart includes his last year's exam notes, flagging rising high blood pressure. Tibby makes a mental note to double check his vitals, listen closely to his heart, and discuss his diet and exercise, all of which could be related to high blood pressure.

Evie pops her head in. "Miracle Worker in the flesh!"

Tibby rolls her eyes. *No miracles performed with these hands.*

"I hear Palmer is exhausted and sleeping a lot this morning at the hospital. Meaghan won't put baby Mila down. And, Bradley has purchased a human-sized teddy bear. How blessed they are that you were at the Christmas Stroll Dinner last night. Things could have gone very badly," Evie says.

"I did what I know how to do," she says. "No miracles. Only my job."

"Okay, Grinchy," Evie reprimands, her brown hair pinned on top of her head in a loose bun. She wears bright green scrubs covered in small Grinches, Maxes, Cindy Lou Whos, and sleighs. "Lighten up. It's Christmas! You ready to get started this morning?"

Tibby smiles at Evie, "You're the Grinchy. Just look at you!"

"Don't you know it! I love me some Grinch…a heart that can grow three sizes," she says, quoting the movie. "I mean, most people these days could benefit from a heart boost of any size."

If Hayes uncovers her mistake, might he find himself a heart that big? "You, Evie Reynolds, have the biggest heart of all. Start bringing our patients back."

"On it!" Evie disappears.

The morning rushes past her. Jewels King has a sinus infection, the result of a viral cold spreading through the Village. Jonathan Shaw slipped last night on a spot of black ice, getting into his car on Main Street after leaving the Stroll Dinner. The x-ray reveals a hairline fracture on his left foot, so she puts him into a boot. Everyone wants to chat about "The Cape's Christmas Baby" and praises her as their own Miracle Worker. "Amazing, Doc Tibby. You were so calm and steady with Palmer. We were worried sick, but watching you eased our nerves." She stiffens at every word.

Ten o'clock arrives before her second cup of coffee, which is likely a huge mistake. She knocks politely on the door of the room where Mr. Whitaker Senior awaits her after Evie takes down his preliminary details. When she swings the door open, she's surprised to be met with not one, but two Jack Whitakers.

"Mr. Whitakers," she jokes, "nice to see you both again this morning. I hadn't realized we'd be meeting so soon."

"Morning, Tibby," Jack says. "Me neither. This morning Dad told me at breakfast he's getting his physical in before the year ended and so I offered to drive him." Jack puts his hand on his father's shoulder. "Make sure he's doing as good as we all suspect before I head out of town again."

Jack Senior touches his son's hand, patting it gently. "I'm great, Jack, really. I can still whoop your butt. Just ask Doc here." They all laugh.

"Pretty sure I'm past the butt whooping age, Dad. And you never did that when I was a kid. But we could give it a go if you like." He winks at his father.

"Well, not here." Jack Senior mocks him.

Tibby's struck by the easy tenderness between them. She jokes, "I wouldn't mind watching you try. But let's do your exam first." They talk through the appointment. His heart sounds good and his blood pressure has come down into a normal range. She recommends he stay on his current medication and do a second follow-up in six months; if it's down further, they can reduce his medicine levels.

"I'm going to let you get dressed and you can open the door when you're ready. I'll drop off your prescription refill. It was great to see you," she nods at both men, "Mr. Whitakers."

"Thanks, Doc," Jack Senior says. As she pulls the door shut, Jack grabs it, holds it open, and slips out into the hallway with her.

"Tibby, you got a moment?" he asks. Her pulse quickens.

"Of course," she says leaning against the hallway wall. "Your dad's really doing great, Jack. He's spry and in great physical condition for his age."

"I'm not worried about my dad."

Her stomach tightens as she reads Jack's expression. "Come with me," she says and leads him into her office.

It's been fifteen years since she was alone in a room with Jack; she rewinds to that night—the night she broke up with him.

THE MEMORY UNFOLDS. SHE IS DEEP INTO HER THIRD year of med school and Jack is immersed in his second startup, his first venture failed. His new app streamlines organizational collaboration, project management, team chats, and shared working files, and gains serious momentum among freelancers and small companies. Investors start to notice. While his partner handles the tech side, Jack's genius is in making what people find difficult beautifully simple. Tibby is beyond proud of him. Together they are growing into the powerhouse team she's always imagined they might be.

After two years of bi-coastal dating, she finds herself pregnant. They've always been careful; but one night over a long weekend Jack surprises her with flowers, two bottles of her favorite Sancerre, and a coveted reservation at Minetta Tavern in Greenwich Village. They never make it to dinner, and instead spend their first twenty-four hours in bed, completely careless. Five weeks later, Tibby stands in the hospital bathroom, leaning against the stall door when two blue lines appear on a plastic stick. Her heart leaps. A fresh energy fills her. She spends the next few weeks methodically contemplating how she can survive residency and raise a newborn. She systematically weighs what she wants from Jack, making a SWOT analysis of their relationship. She decides she wants everything, a whole big beautiful life together with careers and a family. If anyone can have it all, Tibby knows she can.

She tells Lila before Jack. Of course she does. Lila does not disappoint; elation, protectiveness, and support pour out of her. One day, Lila arrives at the Bleeker Street studio with boxes of prenatal vitamins. A week later, Lila attends Tibby's first doctor appointment and takes notes, as if Tibby might not be a real doctor. They both agree news this big must be given in person. She practices how she will tell Jack in front of Lila and both of them are giddy knowing what an amazing father he'll be. When she confesses to Lila her small fear that Jack might flip out and walk away, Lila decisively dismisses the possibility, boosting her confidence. She schedules three days off and buys a plane ticket to Silicon Valley. It's her turn to surprise Jack.

Two days before her scheduled adventure, while working a habitually frenzied night shift and immersed in the mysterious symptoms of a new patient, she ignores the ache in her lower back. When the ache grows into cramping in her lower abdomen, she finally escapes to the restroom. She miscarries leaning against the same hospital bathroom stall walls that first witnessed those two blue lines. Lila holds her on their green velvet couch as she sobs through her grief for three days instead of heading west. Her devastation compounds with the notion that she failed—the baby and Jack, leaving her completely broken and unable to even talk about what happened despite Lila's coaxing. Weeks later, when she finally finds herself in Jack's arms again, the constant reminder of her loss, and her failure, becomes unbearable. She ends their relationship completely, telling Jack she's realized she'll never be ready to settle down. She walks out of his Silicon Valley apartment and never speaks to him again.

UNTIL NOW. TIBBY LEANS AGAINST HER OFFICE WALL, arms crossed, feigning confidence. *What kind of doctor loses her own baby?*

"What can I help you with, Jack?" she asks. She inhales his woody, leather scent, Bleu de Chanel. Her body tingles with a Pavlovian response.

"Are you okay?"

"Of course. Why would you ask?"

"Hayes Carter had some very detailed questions for me last night. Every one of them about you."

She stands up straighter. "What did he ask?"

"He knew we dated. He asked about why we broke up. If you ever talked about leaving New York when we were together. And then he asked what I knew about your time at New York Memorial. Said he knew someone who'd been your patient who had adored you. He asked if I knew why you'd suddenly decided to leave." He leans against her desk, sitting on its edge. "Tibby, what's going on? Why is this guy asking all these questions?"

Who has Hayes spoken with in New York?

"Nothing. Nothing is going on. I told you, I was burned out, so I left New York. Of course his friend adored me—all my patients do." She raises her hand to point out her years of Clinical Excellence Awards as proof, forgetting she's hidden them. "I have no idea why Hayes Carter has shown up on the Cape at Christmas asking all these questions. "

"Have dinner with me."

She jerks backwards. "Jack, no. I can't."

He stands and leans into her. "You always did disappear when things got messy."

"That's not fair, Jack." The heat between them radiates.

"One dinner. Two old friends catching up." He turns to leave, opening her office door.

There's a part of her that doesn't want him to walk out of it—the part that smells Bleu de Chanel. Her body remembers every inch of him. "Okay. One dinner. You're buying."

He smiles. "Henlopen Oyster Bar. Tomorrow at 6 p.m."

"See you tomorrow, Jack." The door closes behind him, her desire flickering to life.

"Doc," Nurse Evie buzzes through the speaker phone on her desk.

She swallows hard. "Yes?"

"Hayes Carter is on the phone for you. Says it's urgent."

She bites back a scream. "Please tell him I'm with a patient. I'll call him back later."

CHAPTER 11

Modern Muse

LILA FEELS THE WARMTH OF NATE'S BODY PRESS AGAINST her. Last night was so intoxicating—a brand-new baby was born, plus rum cake—that by two this morning they finally succumbed to sheer exhaustion, climbing into their downy, cloudlike king and turning off their morning alarms. Was last night enough to erase the invisible barricade recently erected between them? Nate's arms envelop her as he pulls her across the crisp cotton sheets into his arms. He kisses her neck and nibbles on her ear. She feels he's already at attention. Her back arches and an earthy groan slips from her lips. He breathes into her, climbing over her as she opens her thighs and he enters her world completely. She's filled with a heady rush, her eagerness matching his, as they lose themselves in each other. A momentary, familiar reconnection, Charleston and Ellie Winter lost in the fogginess of waking.

"Good morning," he props his head up on his arm, elbow bent, looking down at her.

She beams, "Good morning."

"Last night was good."

"Last night was fantastic, Nate. I mean, we had a baby."

His eyes bulge. "I didn't even know we were pregnant!"

She laughs, pushing his arm to collapse. "You know what I mean."

"I think it was our best Stroll Dinner yet." He kisses her forehead, grabs his cell from his nightstand, and heads into the bathroom. "Next year, we can do a Lowcountry Stroll Dinner in Charleston with an oyster roast and holiday biscuits, Spanish moss, gas lanterns..." His voice trails as he closes the bathroom door.

Her blissful morning amnesia vanishes. *Charleston. Ellie Winter.* Modern Muse. *Hayes Carter.* A nervous energy returns. *I've got to control the narrative.*

Lila grabs her cell from her nightstand and texts Tibby.

How's Palmer? The baby? Also, what incident happened at NYC Memorial that Hayes wants to know about?

Hayes's notes linger in her mind. Three dots bubble up. Then disappear. Then bubble up again.

Palmer and baby are great. No idea. With patients. Talk later this afternoon. 🖤🍼

Lila's fingers hover over the keyboard. She emphasizes Tibby's text with a heart because it would be rude not to. Then types,

I'm doing the interview. Ok to use the guesthouse this afternoon?

So proud of you! Yes, of course.

She exhales. When she read Hayes's notebook last night after receiving Athena's not-so-subtle demand for the *Modern Muse* interview, she realized she has to tell her own story before he does. Her readers deserve to hear the truth directly from her rather than hearing some version from a gossip rag—even a luxury gossip rag like *Park & Fifth*. Coming clean herself might be the only way to keep them.

Lila's phone rings, flashing an old photo of Tibby in scrubs. She picks up immediately. "Do you want me to come? I have patients but I could rearrange a few things if needed."

"No. I need to do this on my own." Lila falls back into her cloud of pillows. "Athena will zoom in, so she will be online with me too. She's waited years for this moment."

"You're going to need some professional hair and makeup. I'm calling Ashley Brimmer at Beach Waves. She did Meaghan's hair over the summer, turned out gorgeous. She owes me a favor for treating her son's broken finger after a Sunday morning soccer game. I'll send her right over to the guesthouse."

"What are you going to tell her? I need professional hair and makeup to pet Bentley by the fire tonight?"

"You're incredulous. Zero faith." Tibby pauses. Lila senses her mentally calculating. "I'll tell her you and Nate are doing a special, separate photo shoot as part of the Sandpiper House's annual Christmas Day photo for some upcoming advertising. I'll say you want to test out her best look beforehand and only have an hour to spare."

She exhales. "Thank you, Tibby. That sounds perfect."

"I'm so proud of you. You've got this! Be yourself and you can't go wrong."

"I will," Lila confirms, nerves already bubbling inside her. "Gotta go, Nate's coming."

Three hours and one Ashley Brimmer zhuzhing later, Lila sits at the white Pottery Barn desk in the corner of the Sandpiper guesthouse with Bentley nestled at her side. She taps her fingers in succession on its wooden top and reviews the pre-screened interview questions and suggested answers Athena sent over this morning, one last time. She's wearing a jewel-toned sapphire dress with cap sleeves and a nipped waist and delicate silver pendant earrings with a coordinating necklace—all chosen according to Athena's firm directive: absolutely no stripes or busy prints. She radiates refined holiday charm. This is how the world will meet Ellie Winter.

Her laptop glows next to a round selfie light and beyond it a cinnamon and firewood scented candle flickers. Nate's gone to the local fishery for inspiration and a last-minute appetizer addition while Tuck prepares fifty chocolate pots de creme. Sloan is prepping linens and guest check-in doesn't begin until 4 p.m. Athena blocks one hour to join her online while Serena Peters at *Modern Muse* questions her by video interview, plenty of time.

Lila's mother's face pops into her mind and she shakes her head, quickly erasing the image as if she's a human Etch A Sketch. She steadies herself with a deep breath, pushing down the gnawing reality that she's about to reveal her most closely guarded secret, changing her life forever. She raises her index finger to her laptop, clicks the red video button on her screen to green, and, at once, appears alongside Serena Peters.

Serena is a class act, exuding sophistication and celebrity. She sparkles in a velvety deep green jacket, a cream blouse, and tailored, high-waisted black pants. After a few pleasantries, she starts right in. "Merry Christmas, viewers! Today, we unwrap the truth, unveiling our twelfth and final day of holiday inspiration. We're speaking with someone many of you don't know, despite her having captured your attention for years." She shifts her focus to Lila. "Welcome. Let's begin with something simple. Who are you?"

Lila's knee bounces. Athena's text pops onto her screen and—as if Athena were sitting beside her, placing a steadying hand on her leg—Lila catches herself and stills. *I can do this.*

"I'm Lila Montgomery. I run a chic inn on the Delaware coast with my boyfriend who is our executive chef, I've never met a throw pillow I don't love, and I believe a great outfit can change your entire mood. I've always been obsessed with creating beauty—whether it's a room, a tablescape, or a moment."

Serena raises an eyebrow and clasps her hands. "You're also Ellie Winter?"

She pauses. Her smile deepens. "Yes, I'm also Ellie Winter. I write spicy holiday romances that women sneak onto their Kindles." Her nerves release. She's in control. She's unexpectedly lighter.

"How did this all begin?" Serena asks delicately, encouraging her story.

"Well, a lot of Bravo TV," Lila says with disarming sweetness. Serena laughs. "I was newly living in New York City, working my first job with an interior design firm out of college. My best friend and roommate was in medical school, so I spent a lot of nights alone on the couch with the *Real Housewives*, *Vanderpump Rules*, and so much more."

"Oh, you're not kidding."

"Nope. I got bored and started spinning my own stories. I wrote a scene. The scene became a chapter. The chapter a book."

"Your first book, *A December to Remember*, had some initial success, but let's say it did not rise to the level of bestseller."

"Not even in the vicinity." Lila nods. "I art directed a gorgeous book cover—we all know a cover is essential for readers to buy a book—and I set up a few online ads early. A couple of book influencers found it. They loved the cover and the story. So, you're correct, not a bestseller, but it did modestly well out of the gate."

"That novel generated the start of a growing fan base."

"It provided a solid foundation for my other novels, yes. And it's still my favorite book."

"It was all inspired by *Real Housewives*? Nothing based on your own life experiences?"

"The Real Housewives have their place, as I mentioned." She glances down at Bentley, searching for the right words. "As a novelist, of course, I borrow emotions, pull from life for the setting, and those quiet what-ifs. Like a lot of writers, I find that fiction gives you the freedom to say things you might not say out loud. Writing can be a way to process something private."

"That definitely sounds like more than TV drama–inspired to me. Is that why you wrote with a pen name? I mean, why keep your identity a secret?"

"Ellie protects me. When I first started writing, I was building my career as an interior designer in New York City, and a reputation as a creative, fashionable, and dependable muse. Ellie isn't me—she is braver, sexier, funnier. She says things I would never. I found it hard to reconcile who I was in my professional life as Lila Montgomery with the boldness of Ellie. When I moved to the Cape and built the Sandpiper House, that extension of who I was remained. What if people who love Lila won't love Ellie and vice versa? Ellie gave me a voice and she also gave me freedom from others' expectations."

Serena's eyes soften.

"So, why reveal yourself now?" Serena asks.

Lila rubs Bentley's head, waking him slightly so his snoring quiets. "I ask my readers to believe in second chances and bold love. I think it's time for me to do the same. The people who matter most in my life deserve the truth. Even if it's messy and scares the hell out of me." *And my hand is being forced.* She fails to mention that she very likely would have declined this interview if Hayes Carter wasn't sitting in her inn right now.

"Well, Merry Christmas and thank you for joining us, Lila. Or should I say Ellie?" Serena smiles for the camera. "I hope our twelfth day of inspiration encourages every woman out there to unwrap her own truth, embrace all of herself, and show up fully in her life. You heard it here on *Modern Muse* first. Ellie Winter is Lila Montgomery. And her new chapter starts now."

"That's a wrap!" someone off-screen shouts.

"Thank you ever so much for hosting Lila," Athena interjects. "Serena, you were absolutely perfect. We're grateful for your exceptional skill to share Lila's story."

"I appreciate the exclusive," Serena replies. "Our holiday series has generated significant online buzz. People are hungry for more and they will adore our twelfth—Ms. Winter." She winks at Lila and Athena. "Going to open a lot of inboxes!"

"We're confirmed this will go live on your YouTube channel and hit social and emails on Christmas morning?" Athena confirms.

"Yep. 12:01 a.m. Happy holidays, ladies!" Serena smiles.

"Thanks so much," Lila chimes in, her stomach beginning to knot. The production crew keeps her on for a while after

Serena signs off as they review the recording, ensuring they don't need a voice over in any spot.

Brilliant! Naughty by Candlelight is bound for #1 with all this attention.

Athena texts her a rare exclamation as she waits.

Thanks Athena. For everything. Ellie Winter and I are grateful to have you on our side. Merry Christmas!

Lila closes her laptop. Her heart still pounding. A string of fairy lights glows against the frost-swept windows of the guesthouse. She exhales, shaky but proud. She's done it; she's taken control of her own narrative. She gathers her things, turns off the selfie light, and blows out the candle, the comforting scent of cinnamon lingering in the air. She packs her laptop into her bag and her phone pings—Nate.

Back from the fishery with some amazing oysters for tonight. Still cleaning the guesthouse?

Lila hesitates, her fingers hovering over the keyboard. She has to tell him.

Finishing up. Back soon.

She hits send, slings her bag over her shoulder, and heads out the door with Bentley trotting beside her. She breathes in the crisp December air and pauses at the Salt & Hearth back door, listening to the voices inside—Nate's and another, familiar one…Hayes. Her heart skips a beat. She freezes, her hand on the doorknob, stopped by the muffled sound of their conversation, unable to make out their words.

She steps inside, Bentley races ahead. Her eyes meet Nate's across the room, his expression unreadable. Hayes flashes his million dollar grin, a knowing glint in his eye. What on earth might Hayes be asking Nate about? If Nate suspects she's Ellie Winter, he might assume Nate is in on it. *I've got to tell Nate!*

"Li," Nate says, his voice tight. "Hayes is telling me about an interesting article he's working on."

"You look astonishingly beautiful today, Lila," Hayes says as if there's no one else in the room except the two of them.

Nate's jaw drops slightly.

Lila's eyes brighten. Her effort to win over the hearts of America's romance readers on screen with a radiant face and long, dark, beachy curls all perfected by Ashley is not lost on Hayes. Nate, on the other hand, fails to notice. Her heart pounds in her chest. She deflects by ignoring him. "Ah, you mean his exposé on the perfect coastal holiday excursions a short trip from New York?

Hayes turns on his heels in her direction and raises his finger in the air. "That's the one. I was getting the backstory on the Christmas Stroll Dinner from the chef himself." Hayes leans in toward Lila and winks, "You'll want to check my notes for those details later."

He is annoyingly irresistible. "Nate says the Christmas Stroll Dinner at Salt & Hearth may be a thing of the past, however, with you two moving to Charleston and all."

Her stomach falls as if she's thrust from a roller coaster's top hat, ninety degrees straight down. Her eyes widen and lock on Nate. What right does he have to make decisions for her? "Nate." Her tongue sharp as if scolding a child.

Nate swoops in grabbing her around the waist. "I only mentioned the possibility. Who knows what will happen." He waves his hand through the air, dismissing Charleston.

"Who knows what will happen" is right.

She steps back from the two men, her mind racing. *Control the narrative.* She considers pulling Nate upstairs into their cottage suite and confessing her double life as Ellie Winter right now, before he hears the truth from Hayes or, worse, sees it on the internet Christmas morning. But telling Nate is an entirely different situation—she's been hiding Ellie Winter from him for years while sharing his bed and building a life together. The thought makes her palms sweat.

"Well, I have some notes to organize this afternoon." Hayes meaningfully taps his notebook against his palm before heading toward the door, his eyes never leaving Lila's face. As he passes her, he leans in slightly. "Brave move today, by the way," he whispers, loud enough only for her to hear.

Her heart stutters. Hayes knows about *Modern Muse.*

CHAPTER 12

All Lit Up

December 22

TIBBY ARRIVES AT THE OYSTER HOUSE FIFTEEN MINUTES early. The restaurant hums with the wild holiday energy required by the Saturday evening before Christmas. The polished copper bar top reflects strings of white lights hanging above. A massive Christmas tree dominates the corner, adorned with oyster and fishing boat ornaments. Determined to mark the evening as a casual dinner between two old friends, she wears dark denim jeans and a black cashmere sweater with suede kitten-heeled boots, and her long blonde hair is gathered in a low ponytail at the nape of her neck.

The hostess slips off her forest green wool coat as Bradley appears from the bar. "Good evening, Tibby." He kisses her on the cheek.

"Bradley," she says surprised to see him. "I didn't expect to see you working this evening."

"Me neither. But Meaghan's at The Hyacinth staying with Palmer and Mila while Aiden, Quinn, and Bella venture out on the *All Lit Up* pub crawl. And it's been a while since I've gotten to spend an evening with my patrons. Between the restaurant on Cape May and redoing Tavern on the Green in New York, I've missed being here. Plus, it's Christmas." He winks. "Any seating preferences?"

"I'll take the table in the back, if you don't mind. For two." She can easily watch the door from there.

"Fabulous," he says, raising an eyebrow in her direction. "You look gorgeous," he pulls her chair out, "but terrified. Who's the lucky guy?"

Tibby laughs, sitting as Bradley hands her a menu. "Just an old friend."

"Whatever you say." A waiter brings him a bottle of wine. Bradley uncorks and pours her a glass. "On the house. Seems like you might need this."

She takes a sip, "Thank you."

"I'll be back." Bradley disappears into the heart of the restaurant, greeting guests at the door, which jingles as they enter. His voice fills the restaurant.

Jack arrives exactly on time. From the door, his eyes find hers. He smiles and moves toward the back table. Her heart skips a beat. It's only adrenaline, she tells herself.

"Good evening, Dr. Harlow," he says, sitting down across from her. "You look gorgeous, as always." He removes his herringbone sport jacket and the charcoal sweater beneath catches the few flecks of silver in his beard.

"You clean up pretty well yourself, Mr. Whitaker." She lifts her glass of wine, grateful for something to do with her hands. "A gift from Bradley. Hope you don't mind I started without you."

"You've always been one step ahead of me." Jack pours himself a glass, raising it with a warm smile. "To old friends."

Her cheeks heat. "To old friends." They fall into easy conversation about Callie, his tech company, her clinic. Callie plays soccer and volleyball. The tech company's acquiring an AI chip maker. The clinic allows her to see all kinds of different people and illnesses, not solely pregnant women. For a moment, she almost forgets why they're really here—the weight of Hayes's questions hangs around her like a noose.

Bradley brings a platter. "Tonight's house special to get you started—After Dark Oysters Rockefeller. Baked East Coast oysters delicately crowned with sautéed spinach and shallots, a touch of Pernod, a splash of cream, then finished with a golden blanket of buttered breadcrumbs and aged Parmesan. Pairs perfectly with the Chablis." He nods at the bottle at the table's center. The dish is both spectacle and sophistication. Bradley sets it between them.

Tibby raises an eyebrow at Bradley, questioning the aphrodisiac he's placed before her and Jack. *We do not need oysters! Just two old friends here!*

Bradley brushes off her look. "Jack, it's great to see you back on the Cape. How long has it been?"

"Too long," Jack replies, shaking Bradley's hand. "Looks like you've done exceedingly well here—hardest reservation in town to land. I hear you're open on Cape May and Central Park soon too? That's pushing the envelope."

"Well, I haven't conquered Silicon Valley, but the restaurants are doing quite well. We weren't sure about Cape May after the summer Meaghan endured, but after a slow start, people are flocking. I'm extremely grateful." He picks up the Chablis, topping off their glasses. "I was sorry to hear about

Rebecca. I can't even imagine what you and Callie have gone through."

"Thank you," Jack looks down at his plate. "Losing Rebecca changed everything—how could it not? The loss was so difficult for Callie, but we're making our way back. That's what she would have wanted."

"It's awful, Jack. Honestly, there aren't words," Tibby says. It's the first time she's spoken with him about Rebecca. "I've seen patients lose their loved ones, it's unbearable. But with a daughter." She shakes her head, lowering her eyes. She wants to tell him about their shared loss, to explain how she understands, at least a little, how he might be feeling. "You seem to be doing okay. I'm glad."

"We all are," Bradley says, placing a hand on Jack's shoulder. "Perhaps it's time for another glass."

"Without a doubt," Jack replies, lightly tapping two fingers against the rim of his wine glass.

The restaurant doors swing open, interrupting the holiday buzz with more jingles. Hayes walks in, surveying the room with Darby clinging to his arm, chattering away. Tibby's glass freezes halfway to her lips.

"Isn't that the journalist staying at Lila's place?" Bradley asks, following her gaze.

She nods stiffly, watching the head hostess lead Hayes and Darby to a table on the opposite side of the restaurant. *Too close. Much too close.*

"He's certainly making the rounds," Jack observes.

"Interviewing the town gossip seems efficient," Bradley says. "Excuse me. I'd like to find out what those two are up to."

"He is thorough," she sets down her glass before spilling any wine.

Jack studies her face. "Tibby, what happened in New York?"

Too much! Too much happened in New York and all of it should stay buried there. "Nothing, Jack. Nothing happened." Her hands tremble as she reaches for an oyster. The luxurious bite bursts with a briny, buttery, herbaceous flavor that melts in her mouth, a welcome, sinful distraction, however fleeting. Bradley makes everything taste like heaven. "Oh my God. You have to try these," she encourages Jack.

Across the room, Hayes looks beyond Darby, surveying the bustling scene, catching her eye. At once, he excuses himself from Darby and beelines directly toward their table.

"Dr. Harlow," his voice smooth as Four Roses bourbon. "What a pleasant surprise."

"Mr. Carter." She crosses her arms and leans back into her velvety high-backed chair, her voice sounding distant to her own ears.

"Jack Whitaker." Jack stands and offers a handshake.

"Of course, Jack," Hayes shakes his hand. "We got to know each other a little the other night at the Christmas Stroll Dinner after all the commotion of the evening." He turns toward her. "I mean, Tibby, you're a true hero. Everyone's talking about the surprise delivery of the Cape's Christmas baby. Miracle Worker, I believe, is the title you've earned."

He's gaslighting me.

Hayes circles his index finger in the air. "You two know each other from New York, right?"

"Actually, we met here one summer. We dated for a while. Tibby was in med school in New York and I was in California," Jack overexplains. Can she kick him under the table?

Hayes nods and turns his full attention to Tibby. "I was hoping we might have a chance to talk while I'm in town. Perhaps tomorrow?"

The restaurant noise fades to a dull roar around her. "About?"

"Your time at New York Memorial." He squints one eye as if peering into her soul, "I think you know why."

Why is Hayes intent on unearthing everything? Is it a basic need to know he's right? Does he want redemption, his old job back? Which of her patients has he been talking with? Who could possibly be holding onto this story besides Hayes? Who would even remember? A nurse. The resident. A hospital administrator or a board member? So many questions; only Hayes has the answers. Maybe she should talk to him.

Jack's hand finds hers under the table, steadying her. "I believe Dr. Harlow is officially on vacation for the holidays," he says firmly. "Perhaps your story can wait."

Hayes smiles, but his eyes narrow. "Some stories have waited long enough."

Before she can respond, Bradley reappears. "Hayes, your date looks lonely. And these two have barely touched their oysters."

Hayes nods, understanding the dismissal. "We'll talk soon, Dr. Harlow. Enjoy your evening."

The room spins. She's suffocating, trying to catch her breath.

"Let's get out of here," Jack says, reading her face. He signals Bradley, who nods in understanding.

"Go. I'll take care of this," Bradley says, squeezing her arm gently.

The Oyster House door opens and, in an instant, the salty, cold air hits her lungs, triggering her to breathe once again like an infant with croup. Jack guides her down the street.

"Walk with me," he says softly.

They pass the Village Christmas tree, glowing colorfully and centered in the bandstand square at the end of Main

Avenue where people gather around. A large group struggles down the street arm-in-arm singing carols—the All Lit Up pub crawl is a smashing success. They head toward the wooden boardwalk, his hand warm against the small of her back. The radiant beach stretches before them, empty and peaceful under a winter moon as white-capped waves drown the holiday music spilling from restaurants and shops.

They walk in silence until they reach a deserted bench facing the blue-black ocean, obscured by the late hour.

She sinks onto it, suddenly exhausted.

"I made a mistake," she whispers, her voice nearly lost in the wind. "A terrible mistake." She looks up at him.

Jack sits down next to her. He's so close, his warmth fills her, illuminating a path forward.

"Tell me," he says simply.

The words pour out of her—the chaotic night at the hospital, the missed diagnosis, Margot Delvy the Senator's wife, the baby she lost. How the hospital neatly covered everything up. Hayes's investigation that pushed too far, likely getting him fired. How she resigned, racked with guilt, escaping to the Cape. Hayes showing up, sniffing around and pushing again now.

Tears fall down her cheeks. "I never told anyone. Not even Lila."

Jack sits quiet for a long moment, his eyes on the dark horizon.

"You know what I remember about you?" he says finally. "How your hands never shake. Not during a fight, not even that night you ended things. Your hands are always steady." He takes her trembling fingers in his.

"We all make mistakes, Tibby. Even brilliant doctors. Even you."

"A woman lost her baby because of me," she says, her voice breaking.

"Yes. Maybe," he acknowledges. "You've been punishing yourself ever since. Living half a life. Hiding who you are."

"Because everyone will know I've failed. Who would want me to be their doctor? I'm a fraud." She slips her fingers from his and buries her face in her hands, elbows on her knees.

"Even doctors make mistakes. You're human. You have to start by forgiving yourself, Tibby." He watches the waves crashing. "Trust me. I've made mistakes too—remember the data breach at Data Works?" Tibby recalls the massive identity theft that impacted several employees following the breach at Jack's first startup. He was consumed with guilt for months, tirelessly trying to make amends for all they'd lost. "We all make mistakes. If you can forgive yourself, others will forgive you too. That's the only way forward."

"I don't deserve forgiveness," she admits.

"Everyone does." He turns to face her fully. "The Tibby I knew would face this head-on. She wouldn't run."

The truth of his words stings worse than the cold. "That's not true. I don't think you fully knew me. I don't think I let you."

"No? Then what changed?" His question pierces.

She slips her hand from his. Her eyes look straight ahead at the lulling sea. "I was pregnant."

"What?"

He's right; I've hidden too much for too long. "I became pregnant. With our child. When we were dating."

"Tibby." He stands up, looking down on her. "What are you saying?"

"We'd been dating a little over a year. I was overjoyed. Ecstatic. But I needed time to figure out what I wanted, how

I could manage residency and a baby. So, I took a few weeks, and figured out that what I wanted was us—all of it, a family, two careers, a life together. Lila helped me come up with a plan to surprise you with the news in California. Then one night, a few days before I was going to fly out to tell you, I was working the late shift. I started feeling poorly, but I ignored that too, until it became impossible to ignore. I lost our baby."

Jack raises his palm to his forehead. "This is a lot to take in, Tibby." He looks out at the sea, adrift in his own emotion.

"I didn't know how to tell you."

"So you broke up with me?" He covers his mouth with his hand. "You disappeared, letting me think I was the problem. That I'd messed everything up."

"Yes. I guess." Her gaze is still locked on the deep ocean.

"I spent years thinking you didn't want me; that something was wrong with me," he tells her.

"I'm sorry. I didn't realize that's what you thought. I was hurt and so very angry with myself. That I had failed us. That I failed our baby."

He stares at the snowy beach before him. "We had a baby." He shakes his head. "A baby."

"For a few weeks, yes." She puts her hand on his back and leans into him. "I'm sorry, Jack. I should have told you."

He turns his head and looks at her. "Yes, you should have. You absolutely should have told me," he says, his words laced with frustrated anger.

Silence falls over them.

He inhales deeply. His voice softens. "But I met Rebecca. She showed me how to love so deeply. We had Callie, who is the greatest gift of all. You'd love her, she's truly amazing. I suppose none of that would have happened if you hadn't broken up with me." The weight of all they never became settles between them.

He grabs her hand. "But knowing there was a baby…our baby…God, Tibby, that's a whole other kind of grief. I hate that you went through that alone, without me."

She wipes her dripping nose with her coat sleeve. "Me too. I'm so sorry, Jack."

"I guess we've both lost things we weren't sure how to hold on to." He envelops her into a warm embrace, grieving something they hadn't known was lost. "But Tibby, you didn't fail. You didn't fail our baby or Margot Delvy's. Sometimes things happen beyond our control. It's a hard lesson, but one I've been forced to learn."

Her mind goes instantly to Rebecca. "No, this is different, Jack. I shouldn't have ignored what was happening. I shouldn't have made either mistake."

Jack cups her face in his hands. "You're human. You're also an amazing doctor. I witnessed you deliver Palmer's baby. Those are the same steady hands I remember." His fingers tighten around hers. "You've been carrying this alone for too long."

His words unburden her. "I don't know how to fix this," she admits something she never thought would cross her lips.

He stands, pulling her gently to her feet. His thumb brushes away a tear. "You start by telling the truth."

The truth—exactly what Hayes is after. But why is he still after it?

She exhales, considering his words, taking a step back away from him. Her Apple Watch buzzes a reminder. Almost 8 p.m. "Oh Jack, I have to go," she says. "There's somewhere I have to be." It's unclear whether it's his immediate, unconditional acceptance of her or perhaps Bradley's After Dark Oysters Rockefeller, but as they stand on this beach where they first met a lifetime ago, Jack Whitaker has never looked more appealing. "Wanna come with me?"

He grabs her hand. "Yes."

CHAPTER 13

Good Luck

THE HOLIDAY MARKET HUMS WITH FESTIVE ENERGY. LAST-minute holiday shoppers bounce between pop-up shops, searching for that perfect gift. The scent of sweet crepes and warm, toasted nuts spill from Powdered Temptation's booth luring in passersby. Carolers stroll the radiant paths that light the evening's darkness, sounding like the next Pentatonix.

Lila and Nate wander hand-in-hand checking off their list of final items needed for Christmas Eve at the Sandpiper House after the annual town parade. Only two items remain—hand-crafted beeswax candles from Wax Poetica designed in a holiday scent reminiscent of Thymes Frasier Fir but with a coastal, salty edge, and fresh bayberry sprigs from the Stem Co. that Lila believes invite good luck, which quite frankly she can't get enough of at the moment. She decides on four large bunches of bayberry sprigs.

It's been two hours since she heard from Tibby—her last text simply said "seated and waiting." She sat on the guestroom bed while Tibby tried on outfits for this evening, which, oddly, presented a dilemma for someone she knows to be exceedingly decisive. Tibby simply hasn't been herself for the past week. But since Jack's surprise debut at the Christmas Stroll Dinner, Tibby seems especially on edge. Is Tibby drowning in too many old feelings? Too many memories long buried and now awakened? *The baby.* She'd made clear that before Tibby left for the evening, she'd be her lifeline. They agreed that Tibby can text her if things go badly, and she will call Tibby with some made up emergency to get her out of there. Phone a friend? So far, nothing.

She holds onto Nate's arm as they walk. "Hey, why don't we pop over to The Oyster House? We could grab a cocktail at the bar."

"Tibby is fine, Li," Nate assures her ignorantly, knowing nothing about the weeks she spent worried sick about Tibby after the miscarriage in New York. That's another thing she's never told Nate—but she rationalizes that detail, partly because Tibby dating Jack preceded Nate and also because that information is not hers to share.

"Sure she is, but I'd love a cocktail anyway." She tries again.

"I'm not feeling The Oyster House." Nate refuses to leave the holiday market. "How about a steaming hot spiked apple cider?"

She gives in. "That'll do." They stroll into The Tipsy Orchard's tent, the top stop at the holiday market. High-top tables covered in bright red table cloths and cozy heat lamps dot the pop-up. At its center stands a Christmas tree decorated with tiny apples glowing with white lights.

"Grab a table. I'll go get us two," Nate tells her.

Lila pulls up a stool and checks her phone.

"Hey Lila!" She hears Ivy's distinct southern drawl approaching. "Holy Bayberry!" Ivy bends down and inhales their sweet scent. "You must be in need of a truck load of good luck."

"Always, Ivy," she deflects. The line for cider is deep. She watches Nate standing next to the Chief chatting, unusually energetic and animated. *What are they talking about?*

"Sugar, I've heard whispers of Nate and some Charleston restaurant deal. Is this what you two were quarreling about on air the other day?" Ivy steals her attention back. "Please tell me you two aren't abandoning us right as the Sandpiper House is becoming the Crown Jewel of the Cape!"

Ivy watches for her reaction. She refuses to give her one. "I don't know what you're talking about, Ivy," she lies. She watches Nate, still chatting with the Chief, when just beyond him, Hayes slips into The Tipsy Orchard through the back with Darby on his arm. Electricity sparks through her entire body. She tracks him to a high-top, his eyes lock on hers, and he flashes that heartbreaking smile. Every inch of her body breathes, freshly awakened.

All at once, everything slides into place around her. The carolers enter the tent, lining up in front of the tree. Familiar faces gather around. The Chief. Goldie and Izzie. Mr. and Mrs. Jenkins. Mr. Grady. Bradley walks in, his arms wrapped around Meaghan from behind, tucking her against his chest as they both take in the scene. Hayes watches her. Tibby surprises her from behind with Jack at her side, raising her cheek to meet Lila's with a kiss. Now here's a couple she isn't expecting to see tonight.

"I guess dinner went well?" Lila whispers in her ear as they greet each other.

"It's a bit of a story."

"Hi, Jack," she says giving him a wave. She wants to steal Tibby, run off and hear every detail right now. Instead, she looks around, noticing that all eyes are on her. "What's going on? Why are you two here?"

Tibby's shoulders rise and lower. "Nate asked me to meet you guys at 8 p.m. I assume for the East Coast's best spiked cider."

Izzie waves at Tibby from across the tent, "Tried the peppermint Nutella crepe yet?"

"Heading there next, sweetheart!" Tibby shouts back, and Jack sweetly smiles at her.

Nate arrives at Lila's side. He sets down their ciders on a high-top and pulls her into the center of the tent in front of the Christmas tree. The carolers burst into the Pentatonix rendition of "Can't Help Falling in Love." He gets down on one knee.

Oh God. Lila freezes. *Is this really happening?* She's weightless as if in a dream. Or is it a nightmare?

Nate takes her hands in his. All eyes focus on them, drawn in by an invisible spotlight.

"Lila Montgomery," Nate begins, his voice steady and emotional. "You've shown me what it means to build something absolutely beautiful together. Something others only wish they could have with the one they love." He's finally pulling the trigger, professing his love with the entire town as his witness. She's overwhelmed with the moment and his sweet words about their love for each other. She nods, unable to speak, only to listen, wishing they were alone. She wipes her wet palms on the thighs of her jeans. "We transformed your grandmother's crumbling beach house into a chic coastal retreat."

Her eyes widen. *He doesn't mean us. He means our business.*

Lila's heart hammers against her ribs as she stares down at him, acutely aware of the expectant faces surrounding them—Tibby, Jack, Ivy, the Chief, dozens of townspeople, and, leaning against a table in the back, Hayes.

"It's official. The Wellington Group confirmed the Charleston deal and I'm accepting. They want us there by February 1," Nate says.

Ivy instinctively slaps her hand on a high-top; she really does know everything.

Nate continues, squeezing Lila's hands tighter. "I can't imagine taking this next step without you by my side. You are meant for me. Together, we are a perfect team. I love you." He reaches into his pocket and pulls out a black leather box with gold trim and a green velvet bow. He flips the box open to reveal a glittering, radiant cut diamond ring set in stunning platinum. "Will you marry me, Li? Will you come to Charleston to build our next chapter together?"

The crowd gasps and murmurs with excitement. Mrs. Jenkins clasps her hands to her chest. Darby and Ivy share a look—a silent *told you so* passes between them.

She's trapped in a spotlight, dozens of eyes watching her expectantly. Her throat tightens. She stares at the ring—gorgeous and not at all what she would have chosen. She looks at Tibby, who grins and nods, encouraging her to accept the proposal she's spent years hoping for. She catches Hayes's gaze across the tent—his expression challenging. A reminder of her secret double life soon to be revealed to the world.

"Yes," she manages, the word escaping before she can fully process it. "Yes, I will marry you."

The tent erupts with cheers. Nate slides the ring onto her finger and pulls her into a long, deep kiss. The carolers break into a version of Bruno Mars's "Marry You." Champagne appears from nowhere. So do honey shortbread cookies infused with sea salt and decorated with a simple heart, the date, and "she said yes." Glasses of champagne are devoured, and the cookies are Instagrammed before they're devoured too.

Tibby rushes forward, enveloping them both in a giant bear hug. "Congratulations, you two!" Tibby steals her hand and inspects her ring. "Gorgeous. Simply gorgeous. Well done, Nate. Finally!"

"Thank you." It's all Lila gets out.

Nate pulls her in and holds her close, whispering how wonderful their Charleston future will be.

Her stomach knots. She feels slightly ill. Is it the excitement? The rush of all she's been waiting for finally on her doorstep? She wishes but knows otherwise. She leans into him. "Nate, there's something I need to tell you." Her heart hammers.

She pulls him away from the celebrating crowd, leading him to The Tipsy Orchard's entrance. Her ring catches the holiday lights dangling from above as she moves through the evening's darkness, sparkling with promises she's not sure she can keep.

They settle onto a small wooden bench tucked near a side garden dusted with snow. "Nate, I need to tell you something I should have told you long ago. You need to know before we go any further." Her voice trembles slightly despite her efforts to steady it.

His face shifts from celebration to concern. "What is it?"

She takes a deep breath. "I'm Ellie Winter."

The words hang between them. Nate's brow furrows in confusion.

"The romance novelist," she continues, her words picking up speed. "I've been writing books under that pen name for years. Since before we met, actually."

Nate's expression hardens as understanding dawns. "The bestselling author everyone's been talking about? The one who writes those spicy holiday romances? That's...you?"

"Yes."

"We've been together for five years. You never told me?"

"I wanted to, so many times." She reaches for his hand. He pulls away. "At first it didn't seem important, we were getting to know each other. And then, it felt too late."

"Too late?" He steps back, creating distance between them. "We share everything, Li. Our home, our business, our bed. And you're living a whole other life?"

"It isn't like that," she insists. "Ellie Winter is my refuge." She puts her hand on his knee.

"A refuge from me, it seems, since you haven't told me about your entire other life all these years." Hurt flashes across his face. His head shakes in disbelief. "How did this even start?"

"I had been dabbling with some stories our first year in New York. Then my first relationship there ended badly—so I wrote it out. My first novel helped me work through the loss of that relationship. It's how I processed this guy who swept me off my feet, falling completely in love with someone else. But then, when you and I met, a few years after, you healed me completely, Nate. You became my safe haven, offering trust and that rush of fresh, mad love."

He crosses his arms over his chest. "What else don't I know about the woman I just asked to marry me?"

Tears threaten. "Nothing. I swear."

Nate runs a hand through his hair, his gaze drifting to the crowds passing by on the other side of the garden, then back to her face. "Our whole relationship, Li. Is it real? Or am I more research for your other books like this first novel? I have to admit I haven't read any Ellie Winter books."

The accusation stings. "That's not fair. Of course our relationship is real. I love you." *Is it enough?*

"Is that why you've been hesitating about Charleston? Because your secret writing career is here?"

"Partly," she admits. "Ellie Winter belongs on Cape Henlopen. Yes, I started her in New York, but Ellie has always been here. The readers, the setting—it's all part of who she is. Of who I am."

"So our future, everything we've built—it comes second to your books?" Nate's expression shifts from confusion to disbelief to hurt. "Charleston is my dream, Lila. What's yours?

"I'm a creative, Nate. I love interior design—the Sandpiper House means the world to me. And yes, I love writing, too—creating characters and worlds. My dreams are to create beauty and invite people into my home, whether in front of a fire or on the page. I want to do both. I need to do both."

"How did we get so far without truly knowing each other? I mean, I've been pretty honest about who I am and what I want. You know ambition drives me. You know I want a Michelin-starred restaurant someday."

"I do know—you've been honest about who you are. This is my fault." She reaches for him. This time he doesn't pull away, but he doesn't respond either. "I need to be honest about who I am before we start a new life together, no matter where we live. I'm sorry it's taken me so long." She sits taller, the truth lengthening her. "I did an on-camera interview with *Modern*

Muse that will air on Christmas morning, revealing that I am Ellie Winter." She drops one last unintentional bomb.

"Oh my God, Lila. Thanks for the heads-up. Is this why you're really telling me now? Before everyone else in the world knows, better tell your..." He looks down at her hand, at the ring now sitting on her finger. His head shakes. "...your fiancé! You said yes to marrying me, but you can't say yes to Charleston? Even though *you* knew about both."

"I want to marry you," she whispers. "But I need you to know all of me first."

Nate shakes his head and steps back, anger now seemingly topping his roller coaster of emotions. "I thought I did."

He stands, turning to leave. "Nate, please—" she calls, torn between the man walking away and the truth of who she is.

"Five years, Lila." Nate's voice is quiet but firm. "Five years of building a life on half-truths. I need to process this." He heads down the snowy pebbled path into the glaring lights of the holiday market.

She stares down at the radiant diamond heavy on her hand, its brilliance catching the holiday lights and casting small rainbows across the snow. Tibby ducks out of The Tipsy Orchard, quickly approaching. "Hey, where's he off to?"

"I told him," she says, her voice barely above a whisper, thick with the weight of all she's unleashed.

"About Ellie?" Tibby asks, her eyes widening as the realization sinks in.

"Yep."

"And he left?" Tibby asks with a hint of trepidation.

"Yep."

"That's not good."

"Nope." She stands. Tibby wraps an arm around her, a lifeline in a sea of uncertainty.

"Give him a few moments to absorb everything. I'm sure he'll come around." Tibby sips her cider; the steamy warmth contrasts with the moment's chill. "I bet he'll be waiting for his fiancée back at your suite. Maybe putting out rose petals all over your bed?"

Lila smiles at the thought. "That would be lovely." She raises an eyebrow at her friend. "I have my doubts. Ellie Winter is a lot to process."

Tibby winks and pulls her closer. "Let's go."

They walk back together into The Tipsy Orchard. Hayes is chatting with Jack, Bradley, and the Chief near the entrance, discussing the Chief's entry in the Christmas Eve Parade as Goldie sneaks up behind The Chief, stealing his spiked cider from his hands and warning him not to overdo things. She avoids Hayes's steely-gray eyes, but he reaches out and grabs her hand. She's dizzy the moment his fingers hold on to hers, a nervous heat pooling within her. "Congratulations, Lila," he says. "Nate's a lucky man." Her breath evaporates from her chest.

"Thank you," she lingers at his side too long.

Tibby pulls her along, gathering in front of the tree. "What are you thinking?"

"Too many things. My head is swirling. I'm engaged! To the man I've wanted to marry for years. But if that man, who loves me so much he wants to spend the rest of his life with me, now questions our entire future after learning I write spicy romance novels under a pen name, I cannot imagine how badly people who don't know me at all will react on Christmas day." She swallows hard. "My mother will be humiliated, and so will I."

Tibby folds Lila's shaking hands into her own. "I disagree," Tibby says. "But if that's truly how you're feeling, there's only one thing to do."

She slowly nods, as if absorbing Tibby's idea by osmosis. "We have to kill the *Modern Muse* story."

"Exactly," Tibby responds.

"I'm not sure, Tibby. Athena's reputation will be tarnished. She'll kill me."

"She'll understand. It's the only thing to do if you really want to keep Ellie Winter under wraps and not #unwrapped."

They lean into each other, foreheads touching, mission accepted.

Lila gathers the Wax Poetica candles and the bayberry bunches, wondering if their magic really works—she is now engaged, but her fiancé has fled. "Okay," Lila agrees. "But how?"

Tibby nods toward the three men double-fisting hot spiked ciders and holding court at the bar in The Tipsy Orchard, Darby on one side, Ivy on the other. "I think we know someone who can help us."

CHAPTER 14

Coastal Confidential, Again

December 23

TIBBY SITS AT THE ROUND TABLE IN IVY BLAKE'S BASEMENT recording studio, a giant microphone looming inches from her face. She taps her fingernails on the tabletop in a restless percussion, taking in the string lights dancing from the ceiling and the fresh pine Christmas tree decorated with gold, silver, and pearl–embossed magnolia flowers—simple, sweet, and very southern. *Why on earth did I agree to this?*

Admitting the truth last night to Jack—about New York, about their baby—unshackles her, leaving her lighter. But the moment is fleeting. This morning, she's putting her mask back on, playing the competent small-town doctor when underneath she's the one who failed her patients in New York. Yes, Jack knows and she's going to tell Lila, who unfortunately remains consumed with her own kind of reckoning, making her timing extremely delicate. But the world cannot know.

"Welcome to another holiday session of *Coastal Confidential, Angels on High* edition." Ivy taps the microphone and winks at Tibby.

Oh God!

She wipes her damp palms on her Veronica Beard black rinsed denim.

"Today I am sitting down with our very own Christmas Angel, Dr. Elizabeth Harlow, and also the dazzling and magnetic duo, hosts of tomorrow's Christmas parade—Hollywood's Meaghan Jones and her partner-in-banter, our very own celebrity restaurateur, Bradley Heartfield," Ivy booms into her microphone.

From the sound booth, Barry plays loud applause over the air. Meaghan overexaggerates a table curtsey while Bradley tosses his navy and green plaid scarf over his shoulder.

Meaghan leans into her microphone and meets Tibby's gaze. "If the parade is half as dramatic as a surprise baby girl born under twinkling lights, we'll be golden." Tibby winces, forcing a smile.

"Tibby, you've become a town celebrity overnight. You're giving Meaghan a run for her money by delivering us the miracle birth we didn't know we needed! Cape Henlopen is buzzing with gratitude. What's it like to be hailed as a hero?" Ivy's accolades turn her stomach.

She shrinks back into her chair. Jack's face flashes through her mind, his expression when she finally told him the truth—not judging but listening, truly listening. He's the exception. How could anyone call her a hero if they knew what she'd done? "Palmer did all the work," she explains. "I simply guided her and was there to welcome beautiful baby Mila into the world. It was truly my honor." She means it.

"How are our mom and baby doing?" Ivy asks, leaning forward with a genuine interest that almost makes Tibby forget the woman's subtle talent for extracting secrets.

"Beautifully. They're home resting," Tibby replies, her lips drawing upwards. "Mila is thriving—all five pounds, eight ounces of her. Palmer is exhausted but radiant. This one barely lets the baby out of her sight." She points in Meaghan's direction.

Meaghan laughs. "I'm practicing my godmother duties. That child will be the most fashionably dressed infant on the Eastern Seaboard. Hell, probably both seaboards."

"And the most spoiled," Bradley adds. "I caught someone ordering a custom-made mobile for the nursery at three this morning."

"Guilty!" Meaghan raises her hand. "Retail therapy usually cures my insomnia. Best medicine ever!"

"Well, Tibby, you are way too modest. Watching you spring to action while panic froze the rest of us was magical! Let's not forget, you left a successful and flourishing career as one of New York City's most preeminent physicians to come to our sleepy coastal town. Listeners are dying to know—what brought you here?"

She knows! It's her worst nightmare; it's not Hayes, it's Ivy with her blaring microphone and addicted audience who will reveal her as a complete and total fraud to the people she cares for more than anything else now. She breathes deeply, to cover for a passing moment to pull herself together. "The answer should be obvious to anyone who loves this town—big city burnout." Tibby sticks with her rehearsed decoy story.

"Totally get that," Meaghan chimes in, picking up her water glass and nodding her agreement at Tibby.

Thank God for Meaghan. "I'm certain you do." She turns to Ivy, "I simply needed a slower pace."

Ivy's head tilts and her eyes lock on Tibby. "Hmm. I suspect there's more to that story. Nobody trades a career at New York Memorial for our little clinic without a compelling reason." Ivy's precision snakes worry through Tibby's heart. How much does she know? "Tibby's gifted us one Christmas story we'll be retelling for years. And tomorrow, the whole town gets its moment to shine at the Christmas Eve Parade—a little less medical drama, a lot more glitter. Who better to steer us through than Hollywood's comeback queen who you'll now find on Broadway and the culinary king himself! Meaghan, Bradley, I hear you two have quite the show planned for us!"

"Absolutely," Bradley chimes in. "We've been privileged to preview several floats this year and all I can say is WOW."

Meaghan tosses her blonde hair behind her shoulder. "I've dared Bradley to wear an elf costume that will make Will Ferrell jealous." She tilts her head in his direction. "Are you accepting, darling?"

"I will not agree to tights," Bradley protests, raising his finger in the air. Laughter returns the room to its lighthearted holiday cheer.

"This is your first year emceeing the parade, Meaghan. How are you leaving your signature mark on this event?"

"Well, for one, I'm matching all proceeds from ticket sales, donating those funds to the Awaken Foundation, which we started over the summer, that works with colleges from across the country to develop and implement transparent standards in the college admissions process. So get your tickets!" Ivy applauds. "And, of course, like all good shows," Meaghan says with a dramatic tone, "we will keep the audience guessing. That's all I'll say."

"Oh, the intrigue! Y'all keep it hotter than the mistletoe gossip at the Sandpiper House. Speaking of surprises," Ivy pivots, "I'd be remiss if we skipped over the beautiful proposal we witnessed last night. Tibby, as Lila Montgomery's best friend, any inside scoop on if we're losing our favorite innkeeping couple to Charleston permanently? I mean, will they keep the Sandpiper open? The Village streets chatter with worry."

She shifts uncomfortably. Ivy knows zero boundaries. "I believe that's Lila and Nate's news to share when they're ready."

"Come now," Ivy persists. "Surely you know whether the Sandpiper House is closing its doors? Nate hinted that we may have already witnessed the very last Christmas Stroll Dinner, surely it can't be true? They can't gift enough panettone to make up for that loss."

"I honestly don't know," Tibby says, which isn't a lie. After Lila's confession to Nate and his horrified reaction, everything's up in the air. "I think they're figuring things out."

"Figuring things out," Ivy repeats, tasting each word. "Seems odd for newly engaged lovebirds."

"Love is complicated, Ivy. Even for picture-perfect couples."

"Now that," Ivy says, eyebrows raised, "sounds like a story." She raises her mulled cider mug in the air, "Cape Henlopen, you've met up with your Christmas Angel, your Broadway Star, and your restaurateur extraordinaire. Could this holiday sparkle any brighter?"

Tibby exhales and her shoulders soften. Only a few more minutes until she escapes this podcast studio that is laced with suffocating questions.

Ivy taps a finger on her headset. Her eyes narrow with a mischievous glint. "But wait, what's Christmas without a surprise gift under the tree? We've got someone calling in right now who undoubtedly is Cape Henlopen's most unexpected newcomer this holiday season. Listeners, say hello to New York City's very own, Mr. Hayes Carter!"

Tibby's stomach drops. Heat returns to her cheeks. Everywhere she goes, Hayes finds her. Only now, maybe she doesn't mind, entirely. She and Lila need his help.

"Thank you, Ivy. Always a pleasure to be a part of *Coastal Confidential.* Cape Henlopen is home to some pretty extraordinary people." Hayes charms listeners everywhere with his smooth, deep, sexy voice and casual compliments. Tibby hears only the cunning edge to his words.

"You're playing with us, Hayes! You've been a mystery since day one, always wooing stories out of everyone and conducting your research." Ivy air quotes the word *research.* "Well, I've done some research of my own. Tell us a bit more about yourself, including that controversial exit from the *Post.* Why did you leave that dream job?

Hayes pauses. Tibby swears she hears him squirm on the other end of the line, but he's barely audible over the pounding of her own chest.

"Simple, Ivy. I disagreed with my editors. When your dream job becomes more of a nightmare, it's time to go. Don't you agree?"

"I sure do. Now tell us, Hayes, what do you think of our Christmas Angel here? She seems to have skipped out on a dream job turned nightmarish burnout too, but you witnessed her angelic hands perform a miracle birth at the Stroll."

Tibby's pulse hammers. The microphone's hum grows loud in her ears. Bradley meets her gaze; he saved her from Hayes last night when she was his dinner guest at The Oyster House, but here he's helpless.

"Well, Ivy," Hayes's voice floats over the airwaves smooth as silk, "Dr. Elizabeth Harlow is one of the most intriguing figures I've come across in my research for this piece. Not simply for her remarkable medical skills, which the town knows all too well after delivering the Cape's very own Christmas Baby, but for reasons beyond her stethoscope. Reasons that began with her remarkable career in New York City, where I first knew her."

Tibby's grip tightens. She dares a quick side look at Meaghan, who sits poised with one leg elegantly crossed over the other, keenly aware of the undercurrent.

"And what might those reasons be?" Ivy digs, her sharp southern attention now locked on Tibby.

Hayes pauses, drawing out the moment like the conductor cueing a final crescendo of Handel's Messiah. "Well I can't tell you that, Ivy. Otherwise, who would read my story?"

Tibby's fear claws its way back up.

"Tibby, can you tell us?"

She sits speechless.

"I think what we're all missing here," Bradley interjects, his voice firm but pleasant, "is that whatever brought Dr. Harlow to our shores is our tremendous gain. Palmer and Mila are home safe because of her skills. I know Miles would be so grateful. As am I."

"Absolutely," Meaghan's hand finds hers under the table, squeezing gently. "I've seen Tibby sit with Palmer for hours, monitoring her condition when her pregnancy became high-risk. I've watched her calm Aiden and Quinn's fears with patience no big city doctor would spare. Trust me, I've met them. Whatever story you think you're chasing, Hayes, the real story is right in front of us—a doctor who shows up. A friend, a support. Some might say, an angel."

Meaghan's words hit her with unexpected force. Is that how they see her? Could they still see her that way if they knew the truth? Jack seems to, although she's not certain. For the first time since leaving New York, she wonders if the life she's built here, the trust she's earned, could be enough for people to overlook her mistakes and see a woman who wants to make things right. Or would they see her as she sees herself…a fraud, a runner, a failure?

"Well, there you have it, Cape Henlopen—miracles, parades, Broadway lights, and maybe even a little mystery sprinkled in. Thank you to our Christmas Angel, Dr. Elizabeth Harlow, and to our dazzling parade hosts Meaghan Jones and Bradley Heartfield, and to Mr. Hayes Carter for that surprise hello. Stay tuned—tomorrow's Christmas Eve Parade is going to light up our little town brighter than the North Star. Until then, darlings—keep your cocoa hot and your secrets hotter."

Tibby pulls the headset off and sets it on the table. Her fingers tremble as she reaches for her phone. "Ivy, can you share Hayes's contact info?"

CHAPTER 15

Maybe, Baby.

NATE REFUSES TO SPEAK TO HER, WHICH DOESN'T SEEM like a great way to start their engagement. He spent last night in Suite 7—the only remaining available suite and regrettably the suite next to Hayes—when they should have been dousing themselves in Veuve Clicquot and attempting the best sex of their last five years. He won't respond to her twenty-five text messages since her Ellie Winter revelation. When she calls, the ringing ends so abruptly that she knows he's hitting the giant red button that immediately throws her into the deep hole of his voicemail inbox. Nate never listens to his voicemail. She wonders if he at least read the automatic transcription. If he did, he's witnessed her repeatedly apologize over the course of nearly two bottles of Cabernet until two this morning. Dry January will be a welcome challenge.

She showers, slips into her black Pistola leather jeans and a cream cashmere sweater, slides on her engagement ring, and heads downstairs with Bentley at her side. Bentley jingles with a fresh tartan plaid bow and a single silver bell around his neck, not so gently announcing their arrival into the foyer. The inn bustles with holiday energy. Guests deliberate on what surprises are in store during the Christmas Eve Parade tomorrow and families button up children into wool coats, heading out for a tea with Mrs. Claus on the holiday square.

She arranges the fresh bayberry stems into two towering cut-glass vases, mixes in a few sprigs of fresh evergreens, and places the arrangements prominently on each end of the front desk ledge, a small beacon of good luck and new beginnings.

Her signature holiday scent fills the air, but it's the light smell of gingerbread that lures her into the Salt & Hearth kitchen. She pours herself a large hazelnut black coffee, hoping to finally find Nate and instead discovering Tuck, who pulls out fresh gingerbreads from several ovens and drizzles them in sweet icing.

"Morning, Tuck," she says, startling him.

"Oh, good morning, Lila! I didn't hear anyone come into the kitchen."

"Have you seen Nate?" She grabs a small plate and an individual-sized potato galette from a tray on the counter. Bentley sits pointedly at her feet, tail wagging across the brick floor, begging-not-begging.

"Not once," he says a bit enraged. "We have an insanely busy day of prep with the parade tomorrow. He was supposed to meet me at six a.m."

She checks her watch. Eleven o'clock. *Where is he?*

She takes an extra-long swallow of coffee followed by three large bites of the galette, because grease is her best friend right now. Her whole body calms. Her headache melts. "I'm sure he won't leave you stranded." She watches him dive into the refrigerator and pull out two trays of bacon-and-rosemary-wrapped petite filets to rest. "Honestly, Tuck, I think you could run this place yourself, no problem."

"Ha!" he exclaims. "Don't tell your fiancé that."

"Secret's safe with me. Let me know if you get in a pinch."

"I sent Sloan to the market to pick up today's fresh order, so I can stay here and manage all this." His hand circles above the ovens. "Hope that's alright."

"Of course. Use Sloan as much as you need today." She tops off her coffee, leaving Tuck to make magic happen all on his own, and winds her way to the Hearth Room in search of Tibby.

Bentley rushes toward Tibby, who stops pacing in front of the fireplace, bending down to greet his sweet face. "Good morning, buddy." She kisses the top of his head and he sprawls out in front of her. Her blonde hair is pulled up into a messy bun, her normally composed demeanor replaced by visible anxiety.

"Hi." Lila exhales at the sight of her best friend. "I can't find Nate. He slept in a different suite last night and won't return my calls or texts." She sips her coffee, "And there's a lot of them." She stands warming her back against the fire, catching her sweater on the end of a few bayberry branches she neatly wove into the evergreen garland draping the hearth last night. A light snow begins to fall outside the window.

"Geez. He must be trying for an Oscar as a drama queen," Tibby responds.

Lila rolls her eyes. "Sarcasm currently not needed."

"Sorry. I'm recovering from an early morning recording of *Coastal Confidential*. And before you ask, yes, Ivy asked about the engagement and whether you two are abandoning us for Charleston entirely. She asked if the Sandpiper House will stay open." Tibby settles into the leather recliner, looking up to finally study Lila. "I told her that was your business, not ours. You didn't bring me a coffee?"

"No, did you ask me for one?" She hands Tibby her coffee mug. "And, thank you—relentless must be Ivy's middle name."

Tibby sips the coffee, a cloud of steamy warmth swirling around her face. "But, are you…abandoning us for Charleston?" Tibby begs. "Asking for a friend." She smiles.

"I don't know! Will he still want to marry me? He's just discovered I am an entirely other person than the woman whose finger he put a ring on last night."

"You're not an entirely other person. You're the same person."

"I can't be sure, because he won't speak to me, but I'm betting Nate doesn't think so."

"Let's skip Nate for the moment. What do you want?" Tibby sips again. "What does your Charleston pros-and-cons list look like? Where is Ellie Winter on that list?"

She raises an eyebrow at Tibby but can't find an answer. A vision flashes in her mind. A new life in Charleston. Having to begin again. Leaving a life she loves. Does she love it more than she loves Nate?

Tibby presses. "If Nate hadn't asked you to marry him in front of your friends and basically the entire Cape, would you still have said yes?"

She hesitates, facing the only mirror she's never been able to avoid—Tibby. "I don't know."

Maybe. I would have said maybe.

"When you write heroines, do they settle?" Tibby asks, her voice gentle but pointed, setting the empty mug on the side table. "Do Ellie Winter's characters choose safe over passionate? Comfortable over true?"

The truth bites at her. "That's not fair. I write fiction. This is reality."

"Maybe, but maybe not. You've spent years writing about women who find their courage, all while burying yours."

Tibby stands, putting both hands on Lila's shoulders. "I think you should figure that out," Tibby says. "You should know what your answer really is, no audience."

Bentley springs up with a bark, rushing toward the glass French doors leading out to the patio. Hayes strides in through them with casual confidence, dressed in dark jeans, a gray cashmere sweater that matches his eyes, and a deep charcoal-colored wool blazer. He stomps the snow off his Red Wings and walks right up to her, standing at her side, eyes darting between hers and Tibby's.

"Good morning, ladies." Hayes meets her gaze. "Well, if it isn't one half of Cape Henlopen's newest power couple," his eyes trail to her ring finger. "Congratulations again on your engagement, Ms. Montgomery."

His brazen confidence sends her heart fluttering. The scent of him—bergamot, cedar, and something darkly masculine—invades her senses. His closeness threatens and tempts. She fights the innate instinct to devour him, deterred by the simple fact that he's out to ruin her.

"I wasn't expecting both of you since Tibby asked me to meet her here. It's a nice surprise," he says.

She takes a step back, regaining her composure. Bentley settles by the fireplace with a contented sigh, oblivious to the tension among them.

"Thanks for coming, Hayes," Tibby begins. "Lila's here because we have a little issue and we think you're the guy who can help resolve it."

"Interesting. I'm here because you two have secrets so scandalous they'll make even a mediocre story—a kind I've never written—go viral." He settles into a wingback chair opposite them. Lila exchanges a glance with Tibby.

Two secrets?

"I need you to help me kill the *Modern Muse* interview," she blurts out.

"What *Modern Muse* interview?" he taunts. "The one during which you reveal you're Ellie Winter?"

"Yes. That interview." She sits in the wingback chair next to his, knees on her elbows. "I made a terrible mistake—I told Nate that I'm Ellie Winter. He..." Her voice catches. "He's devastated. I can't do this to him, not publicly, not on Christmas." She omits that she's desperately worried about what everyone else who hasn't asked her to marry them will think too. *My mother!*

Hayes studies her face. "So you reveal your secret identity to save your relationship, only to want to bury it again to save your relationship." He whistles low. "That's quite the predicament."

She twists her engagement ring, still unfamiliar on her finger.

"Do you have connections at *Modern Muse*?" Tibby interjects.

"Your notebook mentions their editor," Lila adds, and Tibby raises an eyebrow in her direction.

"So you did read my notebook at the Stroll Dinner?" Hayes's eyes narrow at her.

"You left it open on the table, when you always have it on you. You were basically begging me to read it."

"Maybe I was," he says. His eyes flicker mischievously. "Maybe I wanted you to see exactly what I see—a brilliant woman living half her life. Hiding in plain sight."

He disarms her with his words. "You don't know me," she says.

"Don't I?" He leans forward. "I know the writer who creates fearless women who go after exactly what they want. I know the innkeeper who designs every detail to perfection. What I don't know is why Lila Montgomery is so afraid of being both."

His clarity leaves her speechless. How does this man who's been in town only a few days see what Nate hasn't in five years?

Hayes leans back, crossing his arms, and looks to Tibby. "What's in it for me?" He gives a questioning nod. "Why should I help hide your secrets when exposing them is literally my job?"

"Because there's a bigger story," Tibby interjects, her voice suddenly firm. She takes a deep breath. "I'll give you my story. The real one. About what happened at New York Memorial."

Lila turns to Tibby, her mouth open. "What happened at New York Memorial?" She's been waiting patiently for Tibby's true answer. She's tried to decipher through subtle conversations over the past months why Tibby abandoned a prestigious career that for years Lila personally witnessed Tibby sacrifice tirelessly for. She's never gotten even a hint, until now.

Tibby's eyes fix on Hayes. "You want the truth about why I left New York? What I'm really doing on the Cape? I'll tell you everything."

A chill runs down Lila's spine. Tibby's steady demeanor is replaced by a small tremor. A fault line about to break open.

Hayes's expression shifts from skepticism to genuine interest. "I'm listening."

Tibby turns to Lila. "I made a mistake, Li," Tibby says, her voice barely audible. "A patient came in—she was twelve weeks pregnant after a car accident."

Her eyes widen and she reaches for Tibby's hand.

"A resident flagged concerns on her ultrasound," Tibby continues, carefully considering her words. "I didn't investigate further. We were swamped with emergency cases. I missed a rare placental issue." She swallows hard. "She lost the baby. Nearly died herself."

Hayes sits completely still, his journalistic instincts visibly battling something deeper.

"The hospital covered it up. They explained away what happened," Tibby continues. "The couple never knew the truth. The hospital buried the resident's concerns, praised my efforts to save the woman's life. My reputation stayed intact, but I didn't. I failed. I failed my patient, I failed her baby. I couldn't take it, so I resigned and disappeared."

The room goes silent. Only the fire snaps. "All this time, I thought you were burned out," Lila whispers. "I guess...you were. Why didn't you tell me? I'm your best friend. I've never kept anything from you. Not even Ellie Winter."

"I told no one." Tibby's voice breaks. "I couldn't face the reality of what I'd done, myself."

"And that's why I was fired from the *Post*," Hayes says, his voice rough with emotion. "I pushed too hard for the truth. The hospital forced the *Post* to shut down my investigation."

Tibby's face drains of color. "Hayes, I—"

"I knew the truth in New York, but I couldn't prove it." He stands all at once, pacing toward the window. "I bet the woman blames herself, you know. Probably spent years thinking it was something she did."

"Is that who you've been talking with?" Tibby asks. "My patient?"

He rolls his eyes and exhales. "Journalists cannot reveal their sources."

Lila notices something change in him. She moves protectively closer to Tibby. "We all make mistakes, Hayes."

"Absolutely we do." He turns back. "But neglecting something that costs a life—almost two? And letting the blame fall wherever it lands without owning it is another kind of mistake."

"What the hospital chose to do was out of my hands. But, I have no excuse," Tibby says, her voice steadying despite the tears running down her face. "What I did was unforgivable. But I've tried every day since to be worthy of a second chance. And this town gave me one, even if they didn't know they were giving it."

Hayes studies her for a long moment, his expression unreadable. Then he turns to Lila. "And you? Hiding behind a pen name, writing books your fiancé knows nothing about?"

"It's not the same," she says, her voice wavering. "Sorry, but it isn't." She turns to Tibby.

"Isn't it?" Hayes challenges, stepping closer. His eyes drop to her lips for a fraction of a second. "You're afraid of being seen—really seen—for who you are. You're both hiding."

His words land with pinpoint accuracy. All this time she's told herself she's living a double life, when really, she's been living only half of one.

Hayes's gaze moves between them, his internal struggle visible.

"I'll reach out to my contacts; perhaps they can kill the *Modern Muse* piece," he finally says, surprising her. "Only because..." He pauses, looking at Tibby. "Because I need time to think about what to do with your story."

Tibby nods, understanding the gravity of his words.

"Your story," he looks at Lila, "has never been mine to tell. But," Hayes continues, raising his index finger to the air, "you *both* need to stop hiding. The truth has a way of coming out, one way or another." His eyes linger on Lila. "You can't build a life—or a marriage—on fiction."

The weight of his words settles over the room. Bentley stirs from his nap, perhaps sensing the shift in energy.

"Thank you," Lila says softly.

Hayes nods curtly. "I'll make the call. Consider it handled." He turns halfway around on his heels and meets her eyes, "One other thing. I've decided to stay through Christmas. A few guests will join me—everyone wants to experience the magic of a Coastal Christmas. We'll take Suite 7, assuming it's still available."

Is he omnipotent? Nothing slips past Hayes.

"Suite 7 had an unexpected guest last night," she admits, "but I'm certain the suite will be available going forward." Surely Nate will come back to their bed tonight, and if he still resists, she'll move him to their couch if she must.

"Perfect. I'd also like to arrange a private Christmas Eve dinner for five. Is that possible?"

"I'll make certain it is," Lila says with a nod. Hayes could ask her to steal the Hope Diamond at this point, and she'd set out immediately. Anything to keep her interview under wraps. "I'll transform the small library off the dining room and set a table there."

"Wonderful. Thank you." As he turns to leave, he touches her arm with his hand. A warm glow spreads through her entire body. She's lit up by the way he looks at her—like he can see every secret she's ever kept.

She stands breathless, motionless, watching Hayes fade into the crowd gathered in the foyer. She hears their invitations for him to watch the Christmas Eve Parade in their sidewalk booths. He's magnetic; everyone is drawn into his orbit. Her thumb finds her engagement ring, slowly spinning the band around her finger—over and over. It's the heaviest thing she's ever worn.

After Dark Oysters Rockefeller

Ingredients

- 24 live oysters in shell
- 4 tablespoons salted butter
- 2 large shallots finely minced
- ¼ cup Pernod or white wine
- 1 teaspoon salt
- ½ teaspoon pepper
- 10 oz baby spinach
- 12 oz heavy cream
- ½ cup Parmesan cheese, grated
- ½ cup Gruyère cheese, grated
- a pinch of sea salt

Preheat the oven to 375 degrees.

Prepare a baking sheet by covering it with foil and crinkling the foil to create a place to nestle each oyster in its shell.

Clean and rinse the oysters, scrubbing them with a brush to remove debris.

Shuck the oysters! Sounds daunting, but not! Use an oyster knife and a cut-resistant glove. Lay the oyster flat in your hand and hold it in place. Insert the tip of the oyster knife into the "hinge" at the back of the oyster. Carefully twist the edge of the knife to pry the oyster open. Cut the muscle away from the shell by sliding the knife horizontally along the inside top of the shell.

Place the open oysters on the sheet pan, careful not to spill any of their juices.

Melt the butter in a large saute pan over medium heat, careful not to burn. Add the shallots and saute for five minutes until iridescent. Add the Pernod or white wine (I prefer Pernod, but white wine works if you don't have any), salt and pepper, cooking a few minutes to reduce the liquid. Top with the spinach. Once the spinach is wilted, stir it into the mixture, absorbing the liquid. Stir in the cream, half of the Parmesan cheese (1/4 cup), and half of the Gruyere cheese (1/4 cup).

Top each oyster with the mixture, about one tablespoon each. Sprinkle the remaining Parmesan and Gruyère on top.

Bake for 15-20 minutes until bubbly.
Top with sea salt and serve hot.

Additional Notes

Best enjoyed after dark by candlelight. Flirting inevitable. Restraint optional.

CHAPTER 16

A Reckoning

December 24

TIBBY INHALES ONE LAST DRAG OFF HER CIGARETTE, STUBS it out, and slips once more from the alley behind Rise Up onto the Village's Main Street. *One last secret.* She considers that perhaps she can break her smoking habit so she won't need to divulge her vice. She makes a mental note and puts "stop smoking" at the top of her New Year's resolutions. She winds her way through a sea of people as the Christmas parade rolls along.

Warm white lights wrapped around bronzed lamp posts illuminate the snowy evening sky as the sunset reflects over the water. Shop windows sparkle the last of their frosted displays—gingerbread houses, toy trains, oyster shell wreaths. Parents boost mittened children onto their shoulders. Teenagers, with steaming cups of hot cocoa in one hand and their phones in the other, sit on curbs. Couples snuggle under plaid blankets on folding chairs. At the end of the avenue, nestled beside the boardwalk and beach, evergreen garlands twist around the wooden rails of the bandstand, where Meaghan and Bradley announce each float, band, and performer in perfectly entertaining banter.

She scans the crowd and spots Lila standing alone beneath the awning of Weeth Home, the Cape's premier interior design studio, whose front windows look to be lifted straight from the cover of *House Beautiful*, the holiday edition. Even from a distance, she reads the tension in her best friend's posture—shoulders rigid, arms tightly folded. The diamond on her finger catches the holiday lights, flashing like a warning beacon from Lila, who appears completely isolated despite being surrounded by a throng of exuberant parade goers.

"Here's our angel!" Darby surprises her from behind.

Goldie, the Chief's wife and winner of last summer's Christmas in July boat parade over the Fourth, shares a frozen hot chocolate with Darby. "How's our Miracle Worker doing this Christmas Eve?" Goldie asks.

The cigarette's calming effects evaporate. "Hello, ladies. Merry Christmas." She forces a smile. The Christmas Eve Parade joy is welcoming and infectious, but their praise relegates her to feeling like an imposter.

"You've got to be the most talked about person in town this holiday," Darby says. "Loved your spot on *Coastal Confidential*. And we don't believe for one minute you don't have an inside scoop on Lila and Nate's Charleston adventures."

A hand gently touches her shoulder. She turns around. "Jack." A smile blooms across her face. He wears a light scruff, a worn-in navy pea coat, and a scarf. "And Callie!" Her heart brightens. Callie's big brown eyes shine brightly against her bright red puffer jacket and a white beanie.

"Hi, Doc," Callie says. "Merry Christmas."

"Merry Christmas, Callie," Tibby says bending down to meet her face to face. Her mood lightens.

"Duty calls, Doc Tibby. Your presence is requested," Jack rescues her. "Please come with us."

"Alright, then," she says. "See you ladies later."

Jack, Callie, and Tibby walk down the avenue as a brass band in red uniforms plays "Sleigh Ride" from the back of a flatbed truck.

"Oh thank goodness," her shoulders melt down her back. Jack laughs and she lets him guide her and Callie through the crowd toward Lila, who gives them a weak wave when she notices their approach.

"How's baby Mila?" Callie asks Tibby.

"She's doing great, Callie. Gained another pound."

"I'd never seen anything like your delivery. And I've seen a lot of stuff on YouTube."

"I bet you have!" Tibby replies. "But there's nothing quite like the reality of bringing a new life into the world. It's truly remarkable, isn't it?"

"I thought it was kind of gross. There was so much blood—I could see it on all the towels they were bringing through the hallway. I was spying a little from the Hearth Room." Callie shrugs her shoulders in truthful admission. "But she was so tiny." Jack gently smooths Callie's straight brown hair, completely engaged.

"She asked the paramedics if she could hold Mila as they were taking Palmer out to the ambulance," Jack winks at his daughter. "But it was a little too early for that, right?" He looks at Callie, who nods her agreement.

"I bet one day you'll make an exceptional babysitter for Mila," Tibby says.

"Probably." Callie exudes the confidence of untarnished youthfulness. "Dad, can I have five bucks for a peppermint hot chocolate?"

"Sure." Jack pulls out his wallet and hands Callie a ten spot.

"Thanks. I'll be back. It's nice to see you!" Callie waves at Tibby and Jack, then disappears into the crowd.

She and Jack reach Lila, who looks grateful for the company. She pulls Lila into a quick side hug. "You hanging in there?" she asks quietly.

"Barely," Lila admits. "Nate's locked himself in the kitchen at Salt & Hearth. Won't come out, won't talk to me. Says he has to focus on Christmas Eve dinner."

"Men," she mutters with an eye roll. "They get away with dramatic sulking, but expect us to be perfectly composed, otherwise we're drama queens—such a double standard." Jack raises an eyebrow. "Present company excluded."

"Mmm-hmm." He avoids commenting.

"Jack, Callie is delightful." They step back into the quietness under the awning, behind the sea of parade-goers lining the avenue. "Not many twelve-year-olds engage adults in conversation these days. Most have their faces buried in their phones."

He smiles. "She's her mother. Social, outgoing, a generous heart."

"She's you," Tibby reminds him.

He lifts his chin, "A little."

"I told Lila everything, Jack. About New York."

"Good. You did the right thing," he confirms, looking at Lila. "You two are basically sisters. If anyone can help you navigate this, we all know it's Lila." He tilts his head toward Lila, raising his eyebrows.

"And, Li, I told Jack about the baby I lost."

Lila turns to Jack. "It was so long ago," she says, "you deserved to know, Jack. But she couldn't even talk about what had happened back then. It's funny how life turns out."

"We're not the same scared kids we once were," he says.

Tibby shifts from one foot to the other, unexpectedly lighter. She steadies her eyes on Jack. "You knocked some sense into me the other night. Maybe too much sense, because I also told Hayes Carter."

His eyebrow arches. "That's unexpected."

She glances at Lila, who's watching a group of children dance along with the marching band. She can't tell Jack about Ellie Winter—that she needed to give Hayes a story to print so he'd kill the *Modern Muse* interview; that's Lila's story to share when she's ready. "He tried to break the story in New York, but the hospital shut him down. He pushed and lost his job as a result. I think he wanted to know the truth of what happened—if the story he thought was there, was really there. I'm not sure he's going to publish it. But he might."

Jack scratches his jaw. "A little scary, I bet."

"Yes." She shivers. "Someone wise told me recently though that the truth isn't as terrifying when you stop hiding from it. Might be something to that. I'm still considering it."

"Someone wise, huh? Must be a really good guy."

"He's alright," she teases, nudging him. They turn back to the parade. Sleigh bells begin to jingle as Santa's float draws the parade to a close.

"Here he is, the man, the myth, the mistletoe legend himself—Santa Claus!" Bradley's voice booms over the speakers.

"Now, for our final surprise!" Meaghan claps and the crowd swells. "Volunteers are handing out paper lanterns to everyone lining the streets. In a moment, we'll release them together. Everyone wait for Santa's cue!"

Tibby remembers that only months ago, when the press hunted Meaghan, Hollywood and all of America disowned her. Now look at her, starring on Broadway, leading the Christmas Eve Parade. She admitted her mistakes, stopped running from her own truth, came clean with America, and America loves her for it. Admittedly, her sparkling personality, long blonde hair, and legs that go on for days don't hurt. *Could I be so lucky?*

The Village glows with lanterns illuminating the sparkling expanse of wintry evening sky. "May your Christmas be magical and your new year shine as brightly as our sky tonight," Bradley says. "Don't forget to stop by the Rehoboth Beach Volunteer Fire Station Museum for Santa's Christmas After-Party!"

She turns to Jack. "I'm skipping Santa and heading back to the Sandpiper House for dinner with Lila. Would you and Callie like to join us?"

Jack teeters back and forth on his heels. The corners of his mouth curl up as he considers her invitation. "My sister and brother and their families arrive in a couple hours." Her spirit dampens. He looks at her, the corners of his mouth pulling upwards. "So in the meantime, yes, we'd love to."

For a single moment, her heart skitters.

"You're sure?" Lila whispers to her, her voice strained. "It might be awkward with Nate."

"All the more reason to have friends around," Tibby insists. She gives Lila's arm a reassuring squeeze. Lila fidgets with her bag charms. She notices the shadows beneath Lila's eyes, drawn down by the weight of her secret identity and engagement troubles, when she should be celebrating another bestseller.

An hour later, they settle into the back corner booth of Salt & Hearth. Kelly Clarkson's new, expanded holiday album sets an upbeat mood, bathing diners in "Glow." The restaurant shimmers with silver ornaments trimming evergreen boughs, vintage hurricane lamps, and intricate glass snowflakes suspended from the ceiling. Tibby notices Lila's gaze drifting to the firmly closed kitchen doors. When Sloan and Tuck appear through them with everyone's drinks, she studies the predictable disappointment on Lila's face. Then, all at once, a twinkle in Lila's eyes erases all signs of it. She hears Hayes's voice drift into the bistro. *Interesting.*

Hayes follows Sloan, who weaves through seated dinner guests toward the small library where Lila orchestrated a lavish private setting for his Christmas Eve celebration. A striking woman with deep gray-blue eyes follows him. Behind her, a distinguished silver-haired man in a Hackett Mayfair slim cut navy suit is accompanied by two beefy, towering guys flanking him on both sides.

"Is that—?" Lila's voice catches.

"Senator Delvy," Tibby confirms, her throat tightening. "And Margot."

Jack follows their gaze. "Friends of yours?"

"Not exactly," she manages. Her hands shake and Jack covers one with his own. The room begins to spin. How could Hayes bring them here, tonight of all nights? Was this his plan all along? To confront her in person with the woman whose life she wrecked for an even more sensational, viral story?

Hayes looks up, his eyes finding hers across the room. His expression unreadable. When Tibby meets his gaze, his eyes instantly dart to the woman behind him. A chill runs down her spine. This isn't a coincidence; it's a reckoning.

Panic assails her. Her stomach knots. The entire town's angelic praise for delivering their Christmas miracle—baby Mila only days ago right here—rings in her ears. But now the woman whose baby she failed to save stands steps away.

"Did you know they were coming?" she asks Lila.

"I had no idea they would be his guests."

"I can't imagine they'd show up with security detail and not notify the inn," she questions Lila.

"Tibby, I had no idea." Their eyes meet. "Nate."

Margot, dressed impeccably in a deep-green long-sleeve midi dress with a bubble hem, silver heels, and a gathered drawstring clutch, takes in Salt & Hearth on Christmas Eve. As they approach the back of the bistro at the library's threshold, she pauses and leans into Senator Delvy with a whisper, then gives a nod. Hayes circles back to his guests in a huddle. At once, all three turn their eyes on Tibby.

"They're coming over here." Lila swallows hard.

"I can't do this," Tibby whispers, starting to rise. "I need to leave." But it's too late, Margot stands before her. Her entire body stiffens.

"Dr. Harlow?" Margot asks.

Tibby wipes the dampness from her hands with her napkin, sets it on her plate, and stands to greet the Delvys. "Yes, Margot. And Senator." She offers them her hand. "It's a pleasure to see you. Merry Christmas."

"Such a pleasure to see you," Margot returns. "Funny running into you here of all far-and-away places."

"Margot, this is Lila," Hayes says. "The woman I've told you about." Lila's eyebrows furrow. "The Sandpiper House is her inn. She started her interior design career in New York." Senator Delvy slinks backwards as Margot introduces herself to Lila.

"Margot," Lila says clearly, slowly. "It's a pleasure to meet you both. Welcome to the Sandpiper House. And on Christmas Eve no less, we are honored to have you as our guests. I assume you're staying in the extra suite Hayes reserved?"

"Yes, we are—here through Christmas. The Sandpiper House is gorgeous, Lila. You've outdone yourself here. I only wish I had known you in New York—I'm always on the hunt for a fabulous interior designer."

"And this is Jack Whitaker and his daughter Callie." Hayes finishes introductions.

Tibby interjects, "So, what brings you to the Cape for Christmas?"

"Doc Tibby, I thought you knew," Hayes says with his classic mischievous tone, "Margot is my sister."

Her face turns white as her jaw drops. The room tilts. She's thrown off balance. Jack's hand goes to the small of her back, steadying her. Lila touches her arm.

"Your sister?" Tibby's voice is barely a whisper. "Hayes, you never said—"

"I didn't anticipate seeing you all this evening. We were intending to have a quiet Christmas Eve dinner. But since we've run into you tonight, I suppose there's no time like the present." Hayes turns toward his guests, "Margot, Tibby recently told me a story that I think you'd like to hear. Maybe we should all sit down."

"Let's move this reunion somewhere more private," Lila says.

"Callie, why don't you stay here and make sure no one steals our table?" Jack says and Callie agrees.

Lila escorts them into the Hearth Room, shutting the double doors. As they move, Jack stays close to Tibby's side.

Tibby begins. She describes the jumbled events of that night at New York Memorial. The confrontation hits like a storm surging over all barriers—its destruction unknown. Margot's polite greeting devolves into raw devastation.

"You missed the diagnosis?" Margot's voice cracks. "Our baby died because of you?"

Senator Delvy's face hardens. "I should have known when Hayes mentioned a Cape Henlopen doctor with a mysterious past. Is this why you disappeared from New York—you were burying what you did?"

She presses her hands to her cheeks. "The hospital buried the story; I couldn't live with myself. Margot, I am so deeply sorry," she manages, her voice barely audible. "There's no excuse for my mistake. Not the chaos that night, not the overflowing ER—nothing justifies what happened."

"The hospital told us it was unavoidable," Margot whispers. "That no one could have known."

"Maybe. I...I don't know. They protected me. They protected themselves," she admits. "A resident flagged concerns. I didn't investigate further. Your exam was perfectly fine, but perhaps I was arrogant, overconfident. I've carried that guilt every day since."

The Senator's rage erupts. He slams his fists on the table. "You let us blame ourselves for years! Margot has been in therapy, questioning what she did wrong, how she could have caused the death of her own child!"

"Graham, stop," Margot says quietly.

Shame engulfs her. *I've wondered the same thing myself for even longer.*

Hayes steps between them. "Margot needed to know the truth. This is why I brought you here, although I wasn't expecting it tonight." He turns toward her. "You were never going to tell Margot otherwise, were you?"

"Probably not," she confesses, meeting Margot's tear-filled eyes. "I was too afraid."

Jack rises beside her, his presence steady. "I think Tibby has punished herself more than anyone else could. If I know her, and I'm pretty sure I still do, she's spent every day since trying to be worthy of a second chance."

"She's delivered countless babies since," Lila adds. "Including one right here, days ago."

"Our baby didn't get a second chance. Nothing can bring back our child," Senator Delvy spits. "We'll sue the hospital, we'll sue you. I'll make sure everyone knows exactly what kind of doctor you really are—risky, cocky, playing with patients' lives. But more than anything, a phony. You're nothing you pretend to be."

Hayes's gaze wavers. "Graham, this isn't about revenge. Margot deserves to know the truth. That's all I wanted—for my sister to stop blaming herself for what happened."

Tibby's breath catches. "You're not going to publish this story?"

"I never was," Hayes said. "I needed to know—for Margot and for myself. We both lost a lot."

"Well, I understand if you want to press charges," she says quietly to Senator Delvy. "I'll face whatever consequences come. Criminal charges, lawsuits, losing my medical license. I won't fight it."

The room goes silent. Her career, her reputation, and her new life on the Cape—*maybe even a second chance with Jack*—everything hangs in the balance.

"You know the worst part?" Margot finally speaks, her voice hollow. "I've been afraid to try again. Afraid to get pregnant because I thought my body is broken. I thought I am the reason my baby died."

Tibby's heart shatters. "Margot, please—you can have other children. You should. Don't let my mistake rob you of that too."

Margot studies her through tears. "I need time to process this. I mean, how do we move forward?"

"I don't know," she admits. "But I'm done hiding."

Margot turns to her husband. "Graham, we're going back to our room. Now."

Senator Delvy looks like he wants to argue, but his wife's tone stops him.

"This isn't over," he tells Tibby.

Hayes follows them out. The silence deafens.

"Wow. Margot Delvy was your patient that evening. That's one thing you left out, Tibby," Lila says.

"I didn't think 'the who' mattered, honestly."

"You're right, it doesn't."

"We'll, I've ruined Christmas Eve." She rolls her fingers against her thumb, pining for a cigarette.

"What happens now?" Lila asks.

"Now," her voice growing steadier, "I wait. And whatever comes next, I face it."

Lila wraps an arm around her. "I'm proud of you."

"Well, you won't be alone," Jack says.

She meets Jack's gaze. For the first time since leaving New York, there's nowhere left to hide.

CHAPTER 17

Love Triangle

LILA TURNS DOWN THE BEDS ON THE SECOND FLOOR, placing a bouquet of chocolate Christmas trees on each pillow—one white chocolate, one milk chocolate, and one dark. She straightens the red-berried wreath hanging in the window, adjusting it slightly to center its cream bow. She replays the Hearth Room scene in her mind—Tibby confronting her biggest fear, her secret exposed to Margot and Graham Delvy, the most surprising Christmas guests.

Surely, he remembers. Granted, it's been years since they dated—but who forgets sleeping with your interior designer while remodeling your office suite? Possibly, Graham Delvy.

LILA SLIPS INTO THE PAST. GRAHAM IS A NEW YORK STATE Senator, representing the 28th district, including the Upper East Side of Manhattan, Midtown, and parts of Gramercy—a swinging bachelor who seduces voters with his bold initiatives and well-defined jaw line. One night he attends private rooftop parties with the ultra-wealthy—politicians, investment bankers, real estate developers, lobbyists, and art dealers—where caviar, money, and drugs flow lavishly, and the next he's hanging out with the regulars—cab drivers, retail workers, construction guys, and small business owners—at local bars. He combines easy sophistication with a hard-working, down-to-earth determination, attracting a wide swath of factions. Everyone loves Graham Delvy.

And Graham Delvy loves women. Models, movie stars, and Broadway chorus girls—all with some shade of long, flowing hair and endless legs—can be found on his arm at every function he attends. The same woman might reappear for a while, but she never lasts too long. He's the bachelor everyone wants and no one can land. So when Lila stands over Graham's table in his local New York City office, presenting him with five gorgeous fabric options for his new sofa, and Graham invites her to have dinner with him that evening, she absolutely knows better.

He takes her to Augustine, a dimly lit, ultra private bistro in the Beekman Hotel, located in the heart of the Financial District. As they make their way into the restaurant, a multitude of evening stars pouring in through the nine-story glass atrium greets them. She's awestruck. And not only by the stars. The hostess escorts them to a back booth and Lila contemplates whether this might be Graham's regular table, eventually pushing the thought from her mind. They laugh, sharing stories and cocktails, leaning closer into each other as the evening progresses. The conversation is easy; Graham is a charmer. When the check arrives, he invites her up to Turret

Penthouse West, where he's currently residing. They barely make it into the elevator without knocking over the bellboy astutely dressed in a ruby red buttoned jacket and a top hat. Graham unbuttons her blouse and unhooks her bra, cupping her breasts and kissing her neck until the elevator doors open and they spill onto the floor in the penthouse living room.

The sex is untamed. Graham is attentive and generous, his touch precise and intoxicating. She groans and aches with an unrelenting pleasure she's never experienced. She begs him to enter her. When he finally spreads her legs, she's so close already she surrenders within minutes and he joins her. A few moments pass and he's ready again. He brings her to orgasm four more times. Over the next several weeks, he calls and texts during the day, sends her flowers, brings her to his private home in Tuxedo Park in upstate New York for a long weekend. They share dinners and go to art museums a few times a week. He's careful to never take her anywhere too public, avoiding the press. He doesn't invite her to attend public events, but she notices that he doesn't take another woman either. It's her first real relationship in New York and she's instantly head over heels for Graham. She secretly wonders if somehow she's living her own Bravo TV show, or sweeter yet, a Hallmark movie, and so she writes down every moment.

But, on a Friday afternoon in late September, Graham says he has to spend the weekend working, and they don't see each other or speak for three days. When she finally runs into him at his office on Monday, after staging the final accents of his interior redesign, he's polite and apologetic. That's when she knows it's happened. Of course, she expected his fascination wouldn't last too long—after all, he is Graham Delvy. But his withdrawal isn't quite what she envisioned. Rather than the playboy vanishing act she expects to ensue, a simple ghosting of unreturned calls and texts, Graham evolves. He's quiet and kind. They go to lunch, and instead of a regular romp after, he excuses himself back to the office. Over the next two weeks, they see each other less and less, and they never screw. Graham's cavalier demeanor is undone. He's disheveled. Finally, he tells her and it all makes sense. He's met someone. Someone has swept Graham off his feet. Graham Delvy is in love. And, not with Lila.

WITH CHRISTMAS EVE TURN-DOWN SERVICE COMPLETE, Lila heads downstairs to replace the winter white flower arrangements with the wispy pine and berry bouquets she prepared for Christmas day. Passing the bistro doors, Nate's silhouette glows in the kitchen, his shoulders hunched, working dough with force. She winces. He's been in here all night, locked away in silence, obsessively preparing the airy overnight cinnamon rolls that Instagrammers repost continuously throughout the season and the Sandpiper House guests pine for at Christmas brunch. She hears voices from the Hearth Room and steps inside, drawn by the murmur. Hayes leans against the mantel, sleeves rolled, notebook on the table. Margot sits rigidly in a chair. Graham in the wingback beside her holding her hands.

"Oh, I'm sorry. I didn't mean to interrupt. I thought everyone had retired for the evening." She quickly turns to leave.

"We needed a bourbon." Graham stands up and makes his way to the bar cart beyond the piano. He drops a giant square cube from the ice bucket into two handblown glass tumblers and chooses the Woodford. "Did you write a book about me?" he asks, pouring.

She turns back around, looking to Hayes, "You told them?"

"Yes." Hayes crosses his arms. "I told them you're Ellie Winter. That you are a wildly successful romance novelist with several bestsellers. My sister has read them all, apparently." He tilts his head in her direction.

"I love your novels," Margot says softly, eyes still focused straight ahead on the fire.

Graham closes his eyes and inhales. He hands Hayes a tumbler, then reassumes his seat beside Margot.

Hayes plants himself in front of her. The sleeves of his crisp button-down shirt are rolled up perfectly. He swirls the bourbon. "What I didn't know is that you'd had an affair with my brother-in-law."

"Wait a minute," Lila says. "Affair is a strong word."

"You had an affair?" Nate surprises everyone, standing with a tray of warm spiked ciders.

"With me," Graham says and raises his finger in the air.

"You had an affair with Senator Delvy?" Nate sets the tray down on the baby grand piano.

"No. I did not have *an affair* with Graham." She uses air quotes. "We dated. Years ago. In New York. Years before we ever met, Nate."

"But he'd met me," Margot says. "So kind of an affair."

"Everyone stop." Graham asserts his authority. He slides out of his chair and bends down in front of Margot, breaking her gaze, forcing her eyes to meet his. "When I met you, I was seeing Lila. It was casual—I thought it was casual." He looks to Lila for confirmation, but she wears only confusion on her face. He dismisses her, turning back to Margot. "But you, you changed everything, Margot. I fell in love with you instantly. It took me weeks to end things with Lila, and I should've done it sooner."

Margot stiffens. "Were you sleeping with her after we met?"

"No," he exclaims. "I've only ever wanted you. Lila was a mistake of timing. You're my forever."

"I can confirm that," Lila offers. "Graham was obviously smitten with you from the beginning. Broke my heart, I have to admit. But Graham changed for the better almost overnight—his playboy tendencies evaporated, because of you, Margot."

"Why did you never tell me you dated Graham Delvy?" Nate's palm meets his temple. "He's the relationship you wrote your first novel to get over, isn't he?"

Her heart pounds. "Yes. My relationship with Graham was inspiration for my first Ellie Winter novel." She walks to Nate and grabs his hands in hers. "I didn't tell you about Graham because I never told you about Ellie Winter."

"You turned our affair into a novel and sold it as fiction?" Graham asks. "Do you know what the press would do if they knew I was the basis of some smutty romance novel?"

"Honestly, you might get an approval rating bump," Hayes says, taking a drink of his bourbon.

"Hayes!" Margot says as the entire room joins in an eye roll in unison.

"Can we stop calling the three weeks we dated years ago *an affair*?" Her annoyance flares. "It isn't like that. It's fiction. And fiction…" She's interrupted by her phone buzzing on the wooden mantel. She picks it up instinctively.

Hayes's phone buzzes in his pocket.

Her phone's lock screen silently shouts the time at her—12:01 a.m. Their eyes meet. "I thought you killed this story?"

"I did!" His eyes don't leave his phone's inbox. He sets the drink down, running a hand through his hair. "At least, I thought I did."

"I don't think you succeeded," Lila snaps.

All at once, Athena's name flashes across her screen.

The interview is live! Modern Muse offered to pull the piece from publishing yesterday—naturally, I said absolutely not. No idea what sparked that suggestion, but we're past the point of no return now. It's magnificent. You're going all the way. I can feel it. Merry Christmas, Lila.

Lila closes her eyes, breathing deeply to steady herself for what she imagines will come next. *Athena!*

Nate grabs her phone out of her hands, hits play, and watches Lila confess to the world that she's Ellie Winter. "Our guests are watching this right now?" he asks, shaking his head.

"Some of them, probably. Yes," she confesses, watching alongside him. For a moment, she's captivated by the woman on screen—magnetic, spirited, and courageous as she unveils herself to the world. Her mother can go right ahead and die. Ellie Winter is here to stay.

"Why would you do this to us?" Nate says, swirling his hand in the air to encompass Graham Delvy. "Who are you?"

"I'm *Modern Muse*'s twelfth day of holiday inspiration. I'm a creator of beautiful worlds—on the page and in spaces we call home. This is me, Nate."

"This is someone I don't know." He holds up her phone, handing it back to her. "I'm going to plate brunch tomorrow, but then I'm leaving for Charleston. It's where I belong. I know what I want to build there. I thought you did too." His ambition shines brightly, exposing the facade of their relationship. "But now," he shakes his head, "it's clear you've been building something else. Something right here that I know nothing about." His eyes look at his feet, then look up and meet hers. "I. Want. Charleston." He pumps a clawed hand in the air, punctuating each word, grasping for his new conquest.

"I don't," she finally admits.

"Okay," he says. "I'm sorry, Lila."

She stands frozen, watching Nate escape.

Graham offers his hand to Margot, "Come with me. We've had a long day. With a lot of new information. And a lawsuit against Dr. Harlow. It's Christmas Eve and I love you more than anything. We're going to forget about everyone else for tonight. I only want to spend it with you."

Margot smiles at him. "You and me."

"You and me," he says. "We'll see you two in the morning. Goodnight, Hayes. Goodnight, Lila."

Lila collapses onto the sofa, tears filling her eyes. Hayes lingers by the doorway, watching her with an expression she can't quite read.

"Go ahead," she says bitterly. "Tell me how I brought this on myself."

He picks up two spiked ciders from the tray Nate left on the piano and sits across from her, handing her one. He samples his, then leans back. "Is that what you think I'd do?"

"Isn't it? You came here to expose secrets. Well, congratulations."

"I came for the truth," he corrects her. "There's a difference."

He leans in, his elbows on both his knees, holding the bronze hammered mug in his hands. His eyes hold hers. She sees no judgment in them, only understanding. Her heart lightens.

"The problem isn't that you're Ellie Winter," Hayes tells her softly. "It's that you've been hiding her. Hiding yourself."

She looks away. "What would you know about it?"

"I know that to live fully, you have to live in the truth no matter what that truth reveals—a top life lesson from the trenches as a journalist." Her eyes lock onto his. "And I know you deserve better than someone who walks away at the first sign you're more than he imagined."

She raises her palm to her cheeks as they grow warm. She doesn't need a mirror to know how red they've turned.

Damn it. Hayes Carter is good.

CHAPTER 18

Mirrors

December 25

TIBBY WAKES UP IN A HAZY FOG. LAST NIGHT, AFTER stealing a couple pints of Nate's infamous Naughty Nog from the Salt & Hearth walk-in fridge and escaping to her guest cottage—the only location at the Sandpiper where she could for certain avoid Hayes, Margot, and Senator Delvy—she promptly added too much extra rum. She covers her face to block the bright morning sun reflecting off the white snow and then rolls over. The alarm clock on the nightstand reads 10:05.

She's slept for twelve hours. *A real Christmas miracle.*

She taps her phone, which illuminates a screen overrun with notifications. As she egg-nogged herself into a deep Christmas Eve slumber, a video of Tibby confessing to Senator and Margot Delvy the truth about her mistake at New York Memorial was posted to a single TikTok account with 734 followers. Last night, she had been too stunned by the Delvys' presence and too defeated by her own admissions. She had missed Bentley ever so slightly nudging the doors to the Hearth Room open as he wandered in. She missed Sloan peering through the small Bentley-made crack, listening first and then pulling out her phone. She missed Sloan's phone fixed on the large golden rectangular mirror on the back wall, capturing every precisely reflected moment as it unfolded at the other end of the room near the fireplace.

Sloan's sister, who moved from Philly to a townhouse in Greenwich Village four years ago as an influencer intent on marrying an investment banker, watched Tibby's confession at one this morning, immediately reposting the video to her 20,186 followers on Instagram. Hours later, a fashion-loving nurse working the Christmas morning shift at New York Memorial hospital sat in the break room dunking a piece of slightly dried stollen into her gingerbread latte from the twenty-four-hour cafeteria. The nurse never worked with Dr. Elizabeth Harlow, but she didn't need to—the renowned doctor's legacy and the rumors surrounding her swift resignation always circulated. The nurse shared the post to her work group chat, and from there the video spread like an epidemic across Manhattan and beyond.

Tibby's gone viral.

She jolts upright, sitting in bed and thumbing through mentions of herself beside mentions of Senator Delvy on every social media platform. She clicks into one, sees the video, and replays every word of the Hearth Room. As she gets to the part where Senator Delvy claims he will sue her and the hospital, the video is interrupted by her phone ringing—a contact she knows well and hasn't spoken to in eighteen months, the CEO of New York Memorial, Walker Prescott. Her hands shake as she declines the call. *It's Christmas morning, Walker!*

She reads the comments next.

"Unbelievable! She should lose her license."

"This is why we need better oversight and accountability in healthcare! We can't let things like this slide."

"Is she just trying to save her career by playing the 'redemption' angle? Sounds like a PR move to me."

Guilt and fear prick her skin. She shivers. *Everyone knows I'm a fraud.*

She tosses her phone onto the bed, fear fueling her every move. She slips into her gray sweatpants and her favorite *I* ♥ *NYC* hoodie, then pulls on her Uggs, a navy wool coat, and her sunglasses. She passes through the Sandpiper House in search of Lila, which is a mistake. Every set of eyes follows her. The inn staff turn and whisper. Guests glance up from their Christmas tree coffee mugs and plates of sweet-smelling cinnamon rolls with sharp judgment. Even strangers know now. Her phone buzzes with headlines and comments blurring the screen until she shuts it off. She makes her way into a secluded hallway behind the bistro, Nate's kitchen echoing the excitement of Christmas brunch through the wide-planked wooden floorboards. She wants to retreat upstairs to find Lila, but the faint laughter of a family with small children in the breakfast room on Christmas morning overwhelms her with shame. Instead of climbing the stairs, she pushes open the side door and disappears into the cold.

The biting wind hits her instantly. She breathes in the air, salty and clean—a sharp contrast to the Sandpiper's stifling closeness. She moves from the boardwalk down a narrow passage through the glistening sand dunes, her boots crunching a fresh layer of untouched snow beneath her. In the distance, children drag their sleds left by Santa that morning through the snow banks, breaking out into a snowball fight. She walks, replaying the video in her mind, hearing her own voice, cracked and broken. Last night, when confronted with the Delvys, she wanted to stop hiding, but now that the truth is everywhere, she can't escape far enough.

She wanders through the dunes of the Cape until they spill open onto a weathered cobblestone path lined by gently swaying pines. She doesn't know where she's going, only that she needs to go. She travels along the cobblestones, ducking under drooping branches, and then a clearing opens before her—chapel ruins glow in the distance, sitting in perfect silence at the edge of the dunes. As Tibby approaches, she sees the roof is completely gone, leaving the chapel open to the Christmas morning sky. Only four crumbling walls remain. Along their jagged edges, small votive candles flicker, their flames fragile but stubborn against the winter air. An improvised altar fashioned from smoothed driftwood at the far wall draws her in. Worn photographs are tucked among layers of shells and sea glass—the faces of parents, children, lovers lost and remembered.

She finds two votives on a single ledge and places them on the altar—one for the baby she lost, another for Margot's. Her fingers tremble as she strikes the match. She kneels, sorrow and grief welling in her eyes.

"I'm sorry," she whispers. "I should have been better."

"Merry Christmas, Tibby."

Jack's voice startles her. He stands at the chapel entrance, snow falling from a loose ledge dusting his shoulders, a single white votive cradled in his palm. His eyes reflect the candlelight as he approaches, kneeling beside her without hesitation.

"I didn't expect to find you here." He kneels beside her.

"Me neither," she says softly.

"Callie showed me the video this morning," he says quietly. "It's everywhere."

"I know," she manages, her voice barely audible. "The truth I've been running from finally caught up with me."

Jack sets his votive beside hers and strikes a match. "I light one for Rebecca every Christmas," he explains. "When she died, I thought I'd never find my way forward. But Callie needed me. She needed me to be strong. So I had to man up, face my grief head on so I could help her face her own. What we both learned is that our tragedies, and I'd also say our mistakes, don't define us. Instead, it's how we respond to them that does."

The flames hypnotize her; she can't take her eyes off them. "I've spent so long punishing myself, thinking if I worked hard enough, saved enough lives, helped enough people, I would somehow balance the scales."

Jack reaches for her hand, his touch warm against her cold fingers. She erupts like a dam breaking under too much pressure. She falls back, sitting on her heels and burying her face in her palms. Shame and self-recrimination cascade down her cheeks.

He pulls her head gently to his chest, his heartbeat steady like an anchor in the storm of her emotions. "You've always been good enough, Tibby," he whispers against her hair. "The doctor who delivered Mila, the woman who faced Margot with the raw truth when it would have been easier to run—that's who you are. Not perfect. Brave. Brave enough to own your mistakes."

She looks up at him and wipes her eyes with her coat sleeve. "I've missed you," she admits. "Even though I have no right to."

"Ditto." Jack's smile is gentle. "Let's get you back to the Sandpiper House," he says, rising and offering his hand. "It's Christmas."

She takes his hand and stands, wiping her cheeks dry.

Half an hour later, Tibby and Jack walk straight through the front door of the Sandpiper House—no sneaking around the back and no hiding in the guesthouse, where they run right into Lila and Margot.

"Where have you been?" Lila rushes toward her, hanging on and not letting go.

"We were getting some fresh Christmas morning air," Jack says. "Merry Christmas, Lila. Margot." He nods in Margot's direction and smiles."

"Merry Christmas? I'm sure you've seen the video of you last night?" Lila asks.

"Kind of hard to miss," she says.

"Did you see the *Modern Muse* interview posted? It's in inboxes and online everywhere," Lila says.

"What? Now, that I did miss," Tibby says. "Where is Hayes? What happened?"

"I haven't seen Hayes all morning," Lila says. "But Athena is what happened."

"Are you okay?" she asks Lila.

"Yes, I'm okay." Lila turns to Margot, "Margot and I spent some time together, last night. She has something to tell you."

"Can you give Tibby and me a moment alone, please?" Margot asks, her dark hair cascading down her shoulders.

Tibby's heart pounds. She nods, understanding this moment has been inevitable. She invites Margot to sit beside her on the green velvet love seat tucked into the foyer's corner.

"For eighteen months, I've blamed myself. Every night, I replay that accident, wondering what I did wrong. What I ate, what I didn't eat, how I moved, how I didn't move." Her voice cracks. "I convinced myself that I failed our baby."

"Margot—"

"Let me finish." Margot's steely tone silences her. "The therapists tell me it wasn't my fault, but they don't know what you do. They don't know that someone—you—missed something that might have saved our child."

The weight of Margot's words crushes her.

"But here's what's strange," Margot continues, her voice softening slightly. "Watching that video from last night, playing it over and over, witnessing your confession, for the first time in years, my pain eased. The self-blame that's been suffocating me—gone. Because now I know the truth. It wasn't me. It was you."

Tears stream down Tibby's face. "I'm so sorry. I'm so deeply, profoundly sorry."

"I know you are." Margot sighs. "And that makes this complicated. Because seeing your pain, your guilt—I realize you've been carrying this burden too. We've both been drowning in it, only in different ways."

They sit in silence for a moment, two women bound by loss and truth.

"I'm angry," Margot whispers. "I'm furious that your mistake cost me my child. But I'm grateful to finally know that someone else has been holding this pain too. That I haven't been alone in it."

Tibby grabs her hand. "What do you need from me, Margot?" Tibby asks, her voice raw.

"Justice."

All at once, the Hearth Room doors fly open as Graham pushes his way into the foyer, his security detail trailing. He wears a tartan plaid jacket and khakis that scream *Merry Christmas,* perhaps making up for the holiday cheer that's absent from his face. He sees her sitting with Margot and is immediately drawn to Margot's side like a magnet attracting a sword ready for protection. "What are you doing?" he barks at Tibby. "Get away from her."

Jack and Lila overhear Graham and race into the foyer.

"Graham, I asked to speak with Tibby." Margot looks at her husband, who reaches for her hand. "I've blamed myself for years, thinking I lost our baby, our only baby so far. I think Tibby should be held responsible for her mistakes and for covering them up all this time." Margot looks at her phone, vibrating on silent with so many notifications. "But the madness that began early this morning and has only spun further out of control..." She looks firmly at Graham, her eyes pleading. "I can't live like this. I won't do it. Mourning all over again. Reliving every detail—all in public!" She shakes her head. Tears fill her eyes.

Graham holds Margot's gaze as if they're the only two people in the world. "You're right. I could never ask you to do that, no matter how furious I am. We'll do it your way, darling."

"What can I do, Margot?" Tibby asks. She'll do anything to right this ship.

"You need to pay it forward. We built the Delvy Foundation after everything that happened that night. It funds neonatal research, sponsors support groups for grieving mothers, and covers hospital bills for those who are underinsured. You want us to release Graham's lawyers? To silence the headlines? Then you will serve as a silent donor. Your donation will expand our reach and help all kinds of women who walk into those groups feeling like their lives ended the day their babies' lives did."

"Absolutely. I'll do anything to help," Tibby says.

"I'm not finished." Margot's eyes grow fiercer. "I don't ever want you to practice in New York again."

Tibby's eyes widen.

"You owe me this," Margot says firmly. Her eyes meet Graham's. "I have been too afraid to try again. I'm afraid my body will fail another baby. But if it wasn't my fault." She swallows hard. "I want to try for another child." Graham's eyes light up like the Rockefeller Tree. He takes Margot's hand in his. She holds on tightly, turning back to Tibby. "And I don't want to ever run into you in any doctor's office in New York. I don't want to be on edge every time I walk into a practice, nervous I might."

The proposal hangs between them. "That's my justice, Dr. Harlow. What do you say?"

Tibby nods slowly. "Agreed. Margot, you should absolutely try for another baby. And you won't have to risk running into me while doing so."

Margot turns to leave, then pauses. "And for what it's worth, I forgive you. Forgiveness doesn't erase consequences. But I know that holding onto hate will kill me. And maybe you deserve it."

She falls into Graham's arms, and he holds her tightly. He runs his hand down her sleek, straight black hair, his lips resting on top. "Okay," he whispers, his throat tightening too much to get other words out. "Okay."

A sweet spark of jealousy tugs at Tibby's heart. *God, how they love each other.*

"What do you mean, okay?" Lila asks Graham. She knows well enough how Graham operates; they need specifics.

He looks at her. "I'll call off the dogs. We won't sue. I'll make last night's confession video disappear and the headlines have a short shelf life. We'll replace them with something more sensational." Margot turns her head, still buried in Graham's chest, and wipes her tears. "But you've got to pay for this, Tibby, exactly as Margot said."

"Graham," Jack steps forward. "If I may..."

"No," Tibby says, placing her hand on Jack's forearm. "Let me." Jack takes a step back and she stands before Graham and Margot. "I will do everything Margot asks. But you should both know that I have already paid. Sure, I gave up my career, my job, a hospital, and patients I loved in New York, a life I spent years building. And now, I will never go back. But more than that, I've lived with a guilty, tortured heart and countless sleepless nights replaying what I could have done differently, should have done better, to save your baby. And the truth is, I don't know if I could have. I'm not sure anyone could have. Could I have acted differently on the information given me? Yes. Would it have changed the outcome? Maybe. Maybe not. Sometimes, medicine doesn't cure; sometimes it's barely a Band-Aid. We will never know for certain. But one thing I do know is that although not flawless, I am a damn good doctor."

Margot gives a silent nod.

Lila approaches Tibby. "You are a damn good doctor," she tells her. "But the town Facebook group is on fire with that video. There's serious questioning about all of it—what happened, your abilities. There's mention of a possible complaint to the state medical board."

"That's ridiculous," Jack exclaims. "The state medical board?"

"Well, I'm not surprised." Tibby's shoulders shrug. "I would have questions and doubts too."

"Tibby, Cape Henlopen needs you," Lila says. "There's no doubt in my mind. How you care for everyone on the Cape—you go above and beyond. Your career accomplishments speak for themselves. I've witnessed your brilliance time after time. But you're going to have to reassure everyone here."

"I plan to, because I'm not going anywhere," she says.

"Me neither," Lila announces. The corners of Tibby's mouth curl up, and a fresh energy fills her. "But you've got to stop smoking."

Tibby's eyes widen. They both burst into light laughter. Mirrors see everything.

"Deal," Tibby says, wiping at her cheeks. "I'll quit."

"I mean it." Lila loops her arm through Tibby's. "No more hiding behind buildings like a teenager."

"No more hiding behind anything," Tibby agrees.

Graham nods once, crisp and final. "Someone will be in touch with you about the foundation—not us." He guides Margot toward the door. "Let's walk the beach, sweetheart. It's Christmas."

Tibby watches them leave, her chest loosening with absolution—Margot's and her own, finding room to breathe again.

Jack stands beside her, close enough that their shoulders brush. "You good?"

"Getting there." She turns to face him properly. "Thank you. For finding me this morning, even if by accident."

"I'd like to think that Rebecca led me to you this morning." His smile reaches his eyes. "You would have liked her. I have to get back to Callie and my family, who quite possibly have sent out a search patrol for me since I left my phone at home. We'll see you this afternoon at Salt & Hearth?"

"Yes. Can't wait," she says.

"Merry Christmas, Tibby." Jack swallows her into an embrace that feels like home. He kisses her cheek. She lingers a moment too long before stepping back.

"Merry Christmas, Jack."

"Merry Christmas!" Lila says, squeezing her hand. "Come on, Doc. Let's get some coffee before we deal with whatever chaos my interview may have unleashed. My mother has left two voicemails and sent four very long texts."

Tibby follows her best friend toward the kitchen. As she walks through the Sandpiper House, she smiles at the staring eyes that follow her, wishing every one of them a Merry Christmas.

CHAPTER 19

Fireworks

LILA SCHEDULES THE ANNUAL SANDPIPER HOUSE CHRISTMAS photo with Laurel Castro for three that afternoon. The traditional photo includes locals who've feasted on Christmas brunch at Salt & Hearth, the inn's out-of-town guests, and all their staff. Everyone gathers on the Sandpiper House's wide wraparound porch, she and Nate at the center. Lila places each photo, in a silver frame with the year engraved, on top of the grand piano in the Hearth Room. They join other shots from over the summers as guests play bocce ball, do puzzles, and enjoy oysters roasting over a crackling fire.

While watching Nate pack two duffle bags early this morning, she reminds him of the shoot and he assures her he will participate, then head to Charleston right after. "You're not who I thought you were," he tells her as she sits on their bed while he folds jeans and T-shirts—the words stinging but true. She's so much more than she's ever shown him. "We're not who I thought we were. I want Charleston," he blurts out once more, handing her his gray, faded Rehoboth Village lifeguard sweatshirt that she always steals to wear on their early-morning summer runs together. Unsure if he means it as a peace offering or a tacky souvenir from their life together, she hugs him, kisses his cheek, and slips the sweatshirt into her top dresser drawer, only to discover her unused wedding proposal lingerie glowering up at her. She pulls it from her drawer, tossing the failed intoxicant into their bathroom trash can, Nate once again completely oblivious. They agree that keeping up appearances on Christmas will buy them time to figure out how to tell people that instead of getting married, Nate and Lila's beautifully designed relationship is being dismantled.

At two thirty, after her Ashley Brimmer styling, she's so wound up she forgets to breathe—it's as if the *Modern Muse* interview is a corset that's strangling her. She's spent so much time with Margot and searching for Tibby this morning that she's only interacted with a few people, almost all of whom already knew about her double life as Ellie Winter. Except for gold-digging Sloan. Late this morning when she brought Sloan into her office to confront her about Tibby's viral video and relieve her of all her Sandpiper House duties, Sloan said that while she admires Lila's side hustle, the people on Cape Henlopen will never see her the same again. Lila's fears snowballed.

Laurel arrives and begins to set up, moving couches and a few chairs into place. Lila paces the wraparound porch, her boot heels tapping against the aging wood. Bentley paces beside her. The brisk ocean breeze sweeps in from the dunes, carrying the faint scent of salt and pine. Her mind spins like a carousel.

"Lila!" Meaghan pours onto the porch from the foyer, one arm around her daughter Bella and her other hand holding a flute topped off with cranberry mimosa. Bradley follows with baby Mila sweetly slumbering in his arms, her first Christmas and she's the gift. Palmer walks behind him, nestled between her two grown boys, Aiden and Quinn.

Lila's heart pounds as she attempts a smile. "Merry Christmas, everyone."

Meaghan slips her arm from Bella and embraces her with a dazzling smile. "Merry Christmas," Meaghan leans into her, "Ellie Winter! What an amazing surprise! Congratulations to you! You must be over the moon about Ellie Winter's latest achievements. You're on your way to a number one bestseller!"

Her cheeks flush. The corset loosens. "I…I am."

"You should be so proud." Meaghan beams. "You know, I've been dying to meet Ellie Winter. Here you are, this whole time!"

Palmer approaches. "A star in our midst!" she teases and steals Mila from Bradley.

"Look who's a dark horse!" Bradley says, putting his arm around Meaghan. "All this time, Lila. Congratulations." Bentley nuzzles up beside him and demands a petting.

"I don't mean to be too forward or to chat business on Christmas," Meaghan begins but then laughs at herself and waves her hand in the air. "Who am I kidding? I don't care at all." Bradley nods. "Listen, I'd love to option the TV and film rights to your novels. I recently soft launched my own production company—I haven't formally announced yet because I'm in the process of acquiring my first titles. And Ellie Winter's steamy romances would make a great addition. Has anyone acquired those yet? If not, I'm first in line."

Lila's heart leaps—not at the question, which is surprisingly thrilling, but at their unexpected acceptance. "Meaghan, seriously?"

"Seriously! Your novels are meant for Hollywood—and me!" Meaghan laughs as guests begin to gather.

She feels the tension bottled inside her melting away.

"Let's talk this week before I head back to New York."

"That sounds wonderful. I'll let my team at Athena Creative know." The front door swings open as Tibby corrals others outside. Jack follows beside his dad, brother, and sister. Callie trails him, surrounded by her cousins devouring tree-shaped sugar cookies from the dessert trays being passed.

"Why, it's Ms. Ellie Winter!" Mrs. Jenkins grabs her arm, pulling her into an embrace. "Merry Christmas, darling. What a wonderful surprise!"

"OMG! Ellie Winter!" Nurse Evie and her giant heart grab Lila by the shoulders. "I love your stories!"

"Thank you," she responds after picking her jaw up off the floor. "Merry Christmas."

"Everyone start to get into position," Laurel shouts from the brick walkway, leaning on her ladder. "Mr. Grady, that front rocker is yours." Laurel points. "Are you wearing the reindeer antlers this year, Chief?"

Tibby slides her arm through Lila's. "Hello, dear. How are we doing?"

"We are great, Tibby. Actually great. Everyone's thrilled that I'm Ellie Winter. And Meaghan wants to discuss TV and movie rights!"

Tibby winks at her, "Told ya."

"Well, everyone except Nate. Where is Nate?" She looks among the growing crowd on the front porch.

"About that," Tibby says. "We can't find him. Tuck says he hasn't seen him in over an hour."

"Oh God." She takes out her phone and begins to text him. He promised!

From her pocket Tibby pulls a folded notepaper with Lila's name in Nate's handwriting on the front. "We did find this. Under your picture on the baby grand."

Lila opens the note.

> *I can't capture this moment, Lila. We aren't the perfect couple. I'm not sure we ever were. Charleston calls. I'm sorry. XO Nate*

She folds the note back up and slips the paper into her own pocket, the words echoing in her mind as the chatter around her fades to white noise. She excuses herself, slipping away from the buzzing porch. Bentley follows her into the kitchen. A low hum of Christmas music floats through the air—the sound of what should be joy, now hollow. In the middle of the kitchen island sits a panettone perfectly wrapped in golden butcher paper, tied with a black velvet ribbon, and adorned with a sprig of fresh rosemary—the last one, left for her. She clutches the note in her pocket, eyes fixed on the panettone, and sinks to the cold tile. *Nate! He's really gone.*

Five years of building something together, moving from New York, creating a home for themselves and others, building a business and a community, and he leaves her with a note. Not even the courage to show up as he said he would and say goodbye in person. She knows she isn't without blame. But she's pretty certain that a stronger relationship, a meant-to-be relationship, would have survived Ellie Winter and not succumbed to the shiny allure of Charleston.

She looks around—everything is a memory of their shared life. She shudders, and grief consumes her in a tidal wave of emotion. Bentley settles beside Lila, warm and solid. Her tears come silently at first, then grow into deep sobs. Her shoulders shake. Bentley's soft snout nudges her—he knows.

Lila mourns the life she imagined.

Tibby's voice sounds distant. "Hey, hey there." She kneels beside her. "Li, are you okay?"

"Yes, I will be. I needed a second."

"You absolutely do." They sit quietly, not a single word passes between them. Finally, Tibby stands up and picks Lila up off the floor.

She wipes the tears from her face and Tibby embraces her. "We're going to be okay. We have each other. Always have." Tibby squeezes her harder and holds on. "Now, a gentle reminder—you have about a hundred people waiting for you on the porch. Laurel is growing a tad impatient."

Tibby hands her a tissue from the counter. Lila blows her nose like a foghorn. "Jesus, Li." They laugh.

"Let's go," she says. "I'm ready."

On the porch, the crowd shifts into final positions—Palmer cradling baby Mila, Bradley with his arm around Meaghan, Jack with his arm around Callie, standing protectively near Tibby, guests clustering together with bright smiles, and Bentley sitting astutely on the bottom step cued by the treat in Laurel's pocket. All waiting for her to take her place at the center, next to a man who's no longer there.

"Is everyone ready?" Laurel calls out, camera in hand.

"Where's Nate?" Ashley shouts, expecting a special promo photo shoot with Nate and Lila to follow. Her chest tightens. How will she explain his absence?

"He had to step away," Hayes's voice cuts through her panic. She turns to see him emerging from the inn, moving with that easy confidence. His words steady her spinning world. Graham holds Margot's hand, following behind Hayes.

"The show must go on, right?" Meaghan shouts.

"It absolutely must," Hayes says, slapping Graham on the back and stepping into the empty space beside Lila. His presence clears her mind and everything comes into focus.

"Actually," she says, finding her voice, "let's do something a little different this year."

She slips off her engagement ring and slides it into her pocket. The freedom is instant.

"We aren't going for perfection this year," she announces to the group, her voice growing stronger. "I've spent my life trying to be who I thought everyone else wanted me to be. A perfect daughter, perfect interior designer, perfect host, perfect girlfriend...perfect everything. But that's not really me." She turns, and a sea of faces stares back at her, listening with anticipation. "I'm Lila Montgomery *and* I'm Ellie Winter. I write spicy Christmas romance novels—that a lot of you read—and I redesign the Sandpiper House every season because I can't help myself!" Laughter ripples through the crowd. "And if that's too much for some people, then they're not my people."

A loud, joyful whistle pierces through the crowd, igniting a wave of applause and celebration. Someone shouts, "Merry Christmas, Ellie Winter! We LOVE those spicy stories!"

She steps forward and bows, the applause swelling around her. "Thank you," she says, clasping both her hands to her chest. "Now, let's caption this photo *new beginnings*." She steps back into place alongside Hayes.

"Then I'm definitely wearing the reindeer antlers," the Chief shouts.

"Not too much fun, Chief," Tibby responds. "I'm watching you. Keep that heart rate down."

Laurel raises her camera. "Everyone say 'new chapter'!"

"New chapter!" they chorus back. Bentley barks.

The camera clicks, capturing Lila stepping into who she's always been.

Everyone lingers until the sun begins to lower in the clear blue sky. Shouts of "Merry Christmas" fill the air as the crowd disperses. Jonathan and Darby ask Laurel to snap a few pictures of them by the Christmas tree in the Hearth Room. Tibby invites Callie and her cousins to make a hot chocolate in the Salt & Hearth kitchen, likely raiding the secret pantry. Jack smiles listening to their scheming, holding the door open for them as Callie drags Bentley in by his collar. Meaghan invites the Delvys to join them with a fire out on the beach for the Cape's Christmas celebration that starts in an hour.

But Hayes lingers. She stands alone with him on the porch as snow begins to fall, dusting the railing and their shoulders.

"You going to be okay?" he asks quietly.

She looks at him—really looks. The gray-blue eyes that see too much, the mouth that speaks truths she's been afraid to hear, the hands that steady when her world shifts.

"I think I'm going to be better than okay," she realizes.

Hayes steps closer. So close, she tilts her head up to meet his gaze. His hand finds her face. His thumb brushes across her cheek. "Good. Because I have something to tell you."

"What?"

"I think I'm falling for a romance novelist named Ellie Winter. Who also happens to be an incredible woman named Lila Montgomery." His smile is soft, genuine. "All of her."

Her heart hammers against her ribs. "Hayes—"

"I know it's complicated. I know we barely know each other. I know many years ago you dated my brother-in-law." She holds a hand up to silence him. He grabs hold and lowers her hand in his. "But, in my professional opinion, I believe that the best stories start with the most unlikely beginnings."

She reaches up, her fingers thread through his dark wavy hair. "It's exceptionally complicated. I need time. I am ending a five-year relationship. Moments ago I took off my engagement ring."

"You didn't have it on that long," he smiles gently.

"Trust me, I'm aware." She nods. "I need a little time. Even though I'm pretty sure you'll make it hard to wait."

"I'll give you all the time you need. I won't rush you." He pulls her into him. When their lips meet, lust blindsides her. Their kiss fills her with fire. His arms circle her waist, lifting her feet off the ground as she melts into him. The world narrows to only this—his mouth on hers, his hands in her hair, the way he kisses her like she's the answer to a question he's been asking his whole life.

An intoxicating contradiction to the careful, practiced love she shared with Nate.

As they break apart, the first fireworks of the evening light up the sky behind them. "Look," he whispers against her lips, and she turns to see the sky exploding in gold and silver, reflecting off the snow and the ocean.

She doesn't watch the fireworks. She watches the way the light dances in his eyes, the way he looks at her like she's magic.

"You were supposed to ruin me, Hayes Carter," she whispers back.

"Oh I plan to." He smirks.

She rolls her eyes at him as another burst of color fills the Christmas sky.

"When you first showed up here, I was convinced you were going to destroy everything I've built. You made me so angry. The way you saw right through me, asking the questions I didn't want to answer," she admits.

"I'm very good at that," he boasts. "But I've discovered that some things are worth protecting rather than exposing."

Hayes gestures toward the door. "Come on, let's get out of the cold." He wraps his arm around her shoulders, guiding her forward. "Wanna grab a hot chocolate? Perhaps a little whipped cream? You know, I recently read this romance novel where the whipped cream played a starring role."

For the first time, being too much is exactly enough.

She answers without hesitation. "Yes."

CHAPTER 20

Coastal Confidential, One Last Time

January 2

IVY'S PODCAST STUDIO FLASHES *HAPPY NEW YEAR* ON A bright red neon sign above the sound booth, uselessly attempting to distract Tibby, who can't stop reliving the hottest New Year's Eve she's ever spent—this one naked, entangled in her sweaty bed sheets, wrapped in Jack's arms.

He'd unexpectedly shown up at the guesthouse right after midnight to properly tell her goodbye before he and Callie returned to California on New Year's Day. After finishing the Veuve Clicquot Brut Rose bottle she'd started while watching the Times Square ball drop with Lila and discussing how they should keep in touch, Jack leaned in to kiss her farewell on her cheek, and their lips found each other instead. A single kiss igniting a lustful volcano, no longer dormant, waiting to erupt. They devoured each other with hands, mouths, tongues, quickly at first and then slowly as if reintroducing themselves, though clearly no introductions were needed. And although Tibby's not entirely sure what's next with Jack, she is certain that their champagne-laced sex has decisively eliminated her desire for any cigarettes, already checking off one New Year's resolution from her list.

"Good morning, Cape Henlopen—and to all of you tuning in from the breezy corners of our coastline, I'm Ivy Blake, and welcome to our first episode of the new year, *Coastal Confidential: The Morning After Edition*."

The words shock Tibby out of her dreamlike state and back to the real world, where she sits across the table from Ivy. Tibby asked her to be *Coastal Confidential*'s first guest of the new year, of course with the Delvys' blessing after she'd stroked a six figure check to their foundation. The Senator and Margot agreed to allow Tibby her own sound bite—the last one of this story before completely burying the headlines with other news.

"Yes, it's January second," Ivy continues. "The champagne's lost its nerve, the resolutions are already fighting for their lives, and half of this town is praying no one brings up what they said—or who they kissed—at midnight. Bless it."

Her skin pricks. *Or who they slept with!* She smiles faintly at Ivy, who she notices can't seem to take her eyes off Barry in the sound booth. Tibby's eyebrows arch.

"This is the moment when the glitter settles, and the truth comes walking through the door wearing yesterday's mascara. Today, we're talking about truths that didn't fit neatly into last year's headlines. The kind that stings before it sets you straight.

We've got a conversation that has been circling our town for days now—on Facebook groups, around tables at Powdered Temptation, and all along our tinseled main street. And today, we're having that conversation completely live—no prerecording. Before we begin, however, let me clarify: This is not a courtroom. It's a room for context, a little compassion, and quite possibly a clean slate. So pour your second cup of coffee. It's the morning after, y'all."

Ivy looks Tibby square on. "Our first guest is Dr. Elizabeth Harlow, known to many of us as Doc Tibby. We begin this year with a conversation I did not request—a fact that I think matters. Tibby did not ask me for a softball segment; she asked for a microphone, which I think tells you everything you need to know about the woman sitting across from me." A warm smile blooms across Tibby's face. "Tibby, welcome."

"Thank you for having me, once again, Ivy. I appreciate your sharing your microphone."

"What do you want to say to our listeners?"

She clears her throat. "I want to start the year off by telling the truth myself—not some thirty-second version gone viral on the internet. I'm here to share what happened at New York Memorial."

"Well, y'all heard it here. Tibby, before we dive into those details, tell us why today? Why now?"

"Because running hasn't worked. Hiding hasn't worked. And after that video, I realized silence is another kind of lie. So I'm done being silent. If people are going to talk about me, they should at least hear my truth," she says, her tone controlled.

Ivy leans in closer to her. "I respect that deeply. And I think our listeners do too. So let's walk into it. Not the headlines, not the comments, but the truth. You were a leading OB-GYN in

New York. Then came one impossible night—a misdiagnosis followed by tragedy and grief. When you think about that moment now, what do you want people to understand?"

"That I'm human. Medicine isn't always black and white. Sometimes you make the best decision you can with the information you have. I was stretched thin, overwhelmed, and yes—I made a mistake. But I've never been indifferent. I care deeply about what happened. I carry what happened that night with me always and try to make up for it every day since."

Ivy pauses, holding her words in the quiet. "When you left New York, was that escape or survival?"

She stares at her ruby red Christmas coffee mug, still steaming with Ivy's cinnamon hazelnut coffee, considering the question. "Both…really. In so many ways, escape was my only path to survival. I'm a consummate perfectionist. Every corner of that hospital reminded me I had failed someone. I couldn't live with myself or the overwhelming guilt. My best friend was living somewhere I adored, somewhere I could rebuild quieter, somewhere almost no one knew my name. I came here to breathe again. But silence turns out to be suffocating. Something I hadn't realized until recently."

"When the video came out," Ivy says with a nod.

"Ah yes. The video."

"Well, before we continue, I want to bring in someone whose name has been swimming laps around this story."

Tibby sits back in her chair. Her steady heart begins to race. *Hayes? The Delvys?*

Ivy continues. "Our next guest washed up on Cape Henlopen's shores this holiday season, drowning in glitter and searching for gold. Hailing from Pennsylvania and moonlighting at the Sandpiper House until she was let go Christmas morning, Sloan Price is with us in the studio this morning. And while she's knocked over a few Christmas trees racing to be beside the wealthiest bachelors in town, she's most notorious for filming the now viral video of Tibby without her knowledge and releasing it online."

Tibby's jaw hits the table. When she asked to be on *Coastal Confidential*, she thought she'd have the podium. But Ivy simply cannot resist upping the drama factor. *I should have known.*

The studio doors swing open and Sloan walks through them, pulls out a chair, and sits down beside her. "Hello, Tibby." Sloan grins wildly, radiating excitement. She's got a seat at the table.

"Sloan, thank you for joining us." Ivy beams. Tibby glares.

"Of course, Ivy. I'm always happy to be part of the conversation," Sloan says in a polished voice. She crosses her legs with a little too much choreography.

"Sloan, why did you post that video?"

"Well, I believe in transparency. People deserve to know who's providing their medical care. I mean, wouldn't *you* want to know if your doctor had a past?"

Tibby's jaw tightens—not in anger, but in restraint.

"I appreciate that answer. And it's true, no one would have ever known about this incident if you hadn't posted that video, except, of course, Senator and Mrs. Delvy. But transparency tends to be most noble when it isn't tied to clicks, sponsorships, or a brand deal with a cheap phone camera company launching its new magnetic grip and selfie light attachment."

Tibby's shoulders relax. Is Ivy taking this in a direction she didn't expect?

Sloan stiffens. "I don't know what you're implying." Her lips touch, erasing her bright smile.

"I'm not implying anything. I'm simply stating the facts." Ivy looks again at Barry, who gives her a wink. "Your post was monetized within hours of going live. Your caption 'You won't BELIEVE this doctor's past—double eyes emoji' feels less about integrity and more about eye-catching headlines—something I know quite a bit about, darlin'."

Sloan blinks. She tucks a strand of hair behind her ear, her hand trembling slightly.

"I thought people would want the truth. That's all."

"And do you know the truth?"

"Yes, I do. I think the truth is pretty obvious in that video."

"Really? I'm not so sure. Maybe you just captured a sliver of something? Something you thought you could get paid for." A stunned silence hums across the studio. Ivy pursues Sloan with a relentless on-air persecution that Tibby expected Ivy would save for her.

Sloan exhales through her nose, which flares in cornered annoyance.

"Look, I'm building a career here. A platform—something I think *you* know about. I have goals. And sometimes in this world, you have to put yourself out there if you want to get ahead. I knew something I thought everyone should know and would want to know. Turns out they do."

The comment hangs heavy. Tibby sits composed, awaiting Ivy's next move.

"Sloan, 'getting ahead' is a fine thing. I can appreciate that completely. But stepping on someone else's neck to do it with half a story is simply opportunism with a ring light." Sloan's cheeks flush. "When you posted that video, did you reach out to Tibby first? Ask for context? Invite her to speak for herself?"

"No."

"Did you consider the harm? The impact on her patients? Her reputation? Her safety?"

Sloan swallows. "No." Her posture collapses, a slip in her armor.

Tibby interrupts. "Ivy, if I may."

"Absolutely, sweetheart."

"Sloan, I won't pretend to understand all the reasons you posted that video, although it seems mostly for money and influence. But whatever the reason, you're trying to expose me as a monster. I am not a monster. I am a phenomenal doctor, one who is human and can make a mistake. What you exposed instead was a moment."

"Well, it seems like a very bad moment, Tibby," Sloan snaps back. "Especially for the Delvys. I think they'd agree that over the..." Sloan is instantly distracted by Barry, who waves his arms up and down over his head from the sound booth. Ivy raises her questioning eyebrows in his direction. He nods and gives two thumbs up high into the air. Ivy holds a finger to her ear, where Barry speaks into her headphones as a grin blooms across her face.

"Listeners, I have to interrupt. *Coastal Confidential: The Morning After Edition* is getting spicier than that Old Bay Bloody Mary you've secretly been sipping this morning—hair of the dog, y'all! This unexpected caller is surprising us all the way from New York City. You've seen the name attached to more headlines than most. Mr. Walker Prescott, CEO of New York Memorial Hospital, you're live on *Coastal Confidential.* Good morning."

Tibby goes perfectly still. Her hand involuntarily tightens around the arm of her chair. She recalls Christmas morning, Walker's name flashing across her caller ID. She threw him to voicemail wasteland, completely forgetting to return his call as the morning spiraled. Oh, how she wishes she had now.

"Good morning, Ivy. Good morning, Dr. Harlow." Walker's voice booms through the studio, large and confident.

"Mr. Prescott, we appreciate you being available to join us. This story has taken on a life of its own here in Cape Henlopen. What moved you to pick up the phone today?"

"Well, you might imagine that since the video broke the internet, I've been paying attention to what's transpiring on the Cape. When I heard Tibby would be live this morning, I tuned in. And, after what I've heard so far, I owe Dr. Harlow more than my silence."

Sloan shifts in her seat, visibly uncomfortable.

"Well, you've got the microphone, sir. What do you want to say to Dr. Harlow?"

Tibby envisions Walker seated behind his antique wooden desk on the thirty-first floor of New York Memorial, fingers tented with his palms nearly touching as he stares out the large glass wall of windows over the city twinkling below him. *Yes, Walker, what do you have to say?*

"As is hospital protocol, we conducted an internal investigation into Dr. Harlow's case—one that lasted a couple months and one that I believe Dr. Harlow herself may never have been aware of. After all, she resigned her position weeks earlier. That investigation was inconclusive."

The studio feels electric. Ivy's posture shifts. "Translate that for us regular folks, Mr. Prescott."

"We found no evidence of negligence. No pattern of misconduct. In fact, several senior physicians who were given the case anonymously to analyze defended Dr. Harlow's judgment that night, citing the ambiguity of all initial test results when considered together with the regular physical exam."

Tibby's eyes close for a single, stunned second.

"Then why, Mr. Prescott, did you allow Dr. Harlow to resign?" Ivy presses.

Walker pauses, long and heavy. "The board was concerned about optics. We were facing simultaneous media scrutiny on other issues. The idea of a high-profile case involving a prominent family terrified them. When Dr. Harlow offered her resignation, begging to go quietly, the board accepted, believing her resignation to be the 'cleanest option' for everyone."

Sloan's face drains of color.

"Did the hospital pay a media outlet to keep the story out of the headlines?" Ivy goes there.

"I have no knowledge of that nor would I ever participate in such things." Walker stands tall, pleading the fifth. "But I will say that in this city, purchasing a story to kill it is not uncommon."

"The vault," Ivy confirms. "Now there's a key I'd love to get my southern hands on!"

Tibby hears Walker rolling his eyes on the other end of the line.

"I'll say something else—something I have not said publicly." He sidesteps Ivy's sand trap, luring her beyond it. "I believed at the time that it was the right decision for the hospital. But I did not consider whether it was the right decision for Dr. Harlow or for Senator Delvy and his wife. For that, I am truly sorry."

Tibby's breath breaks, soft and shocked. She retains her composure.

"Mr. Prescott, that's a significant admission," Ivy clarifies.

"It's overdue. Dr. Harlow carried the entire weight of that tragedy alone, even when the investigation did not place the blame solely on her shoulders. She deserves better."

"What would you say to those who've watched ten seconds of footage and decided they know the whole of Dr. Harlow's career?"

"I would say that ten seconds does not define a physician who spent years saving lives and delivering new ones. I would ask them to consider whether they want a world where the mistakes they make are a permanent sentence."

Sloan flinches.

Walker's voice softens. "Elizabeth, I hope someday you can forgive the way things unfolded. You were not alone in that room."

Tibby swallows hard, eyes glistening.

"Thank you, Walker. That means more than you know."

"Mr. Prescott, thank you for calling in. We appreciate your candor."

"Thank you, Ivy. And good luck, Dr. Harlow."

The call clicks off. Ivy allows an unprecedented moment of silence as vindication settles around them. "Well, y'all, one thing I know to be true—the morning after is when most of us realize what we wish we'd done differently.

"Tibby, folks around town have been debating whether Sloan's video warrants questioning your competence as a doctor. I have zero doubt that you're not only an outstanding physician, but you're meant to be here with us on the Cape. You elevate our community—you heal us physically and offer warmth and companionship to countless people. Cape Henlopen is where you belong; I pray you'll remain."

"I'm not going anywhere, Ivy. I'm reopening my clinic hours starting next week."

"I'll be making my annual check-up appointment on Monday!" Ivy announces. "What we heard today isn't gossip or scandal, but something we don't get nearly enough of—context and courage. We must remember that a mistake is not a life sentence. A moment is not a whole story. In this new year, I hope we can practice being slower to judge and quicker to listen."

Tibby's phone vibrates on silent. "Thank you for having me, Ivy."

"Me too," Sloan says. "And I stand behind putting that video out. People need to know."

"I think they do now," Tibby says.

"Ditto." Ivy winks at Tibby. "Now, before I let everyone go, one last note for your calendars. Tomorrow afternoon at the Sandpiper House our very own Lila Montgomery—a.k.a. Ms. Ellie Winter—will give us an exclusive sneak peek of her upcoming novel, *Unwrapping Us,* which I predict will be her steamiest yet. It's her very first book signing and reading. See you there, Cape Henlopen! Remember, keep your cocoa hot and your secrets hotter."

Barry gives the all clear. Ivy rises, extending her hand. "Thank you, Tibby. For your courage. For your honesty. Redemption is messy but beautiful. Also a ratings magnet!"

"Thank you, Ivy." Tibby shakes her hand. "Sloan, good luck to you." Tibby steps into the studio lobby, where Lila sits waiting.

Lila rises from the studio lobby chair, her eyes bright with pride, and sweeps her into a hug. Her eyes glisten, grateful for Lila's unwavering support. The shared history between them pulses, unspoken but understood.

Lila releases her, taking a step back to survey her friend. "You've done it again. The Cape's Facebook group is on fire once more. Everyone agrees with Ivy, no need for an inquiry request. I think your calendar's going to be full."

She breathes in deeply, then slowly exhales the weight of other people's opinions. "Anything less wouldn't be me, I suppose."

"Hayes called."

"Of course he did." Tibby smirks. "How many times has he called today?"

"Only twice." Lila tilts her head and raises one shoulder to her chin, making a sugary expression. "What? He's helping us get the word out in New York City that Tuck needs a sous chef. But that's not why he called. Apparently, Graham and Margot listened in. They're sitting down with Walker Prescott this afternoon. I guess Graham has a few things he wants to clear up with Walker before the dust settles."

Tibby's lips form a silent "o." She takes her navy wool coat from Lila.

"And...the vault?!" Lila exclaims, slipping on her own burgundy cashmere wrap.

"I know. I mean, I'd heard the rumors..." Tibby says, pulling on her gloves.

Sloan opens the studio door into the lobby, her ear glued to her cell, deep in conversation and seemingly unfazed by what transpired only moments ago on *Coastal Confidential.* She looks at Tibby and Lila, giving them a nod. "Ladies," she says, then climbs the velvety green stairs.

"I hope those take her far away from here."

"I'm guessing Sloan is on to much bigger things. Or at least she thinks so," Lila says. Their laughter mingles with Ivy's holiday outro music still playing dimly in the background. "Let's go."

They venture out into the crisp morning air. Snow dusts the grand porch, where mistletoe still hangs over the doorway. They traverse the cobblestones, winding down into the heart of the Village where hazelnut coffee, cinnamon French toast, and, most likely, tables full of *Coastal Confidential* listeners await them at Powdered Temptation. The ocean murmurs in the distance.

Tibby's phone buzzes again. She opens her messages, where Jack's words stare back at her. Her body radiates with a slow warmth.

That was some morning after. 😉 Proud of you.

She laughs out loud, knowing exactly which morning after he means. She plays along.

Agreed. 🥂🔥😉 It feels good to be honest about who I am. Mostly, with myself.

Callie wants to come back for spring break. I'm thinking I might tag along. Dinner at The Oyster House? All the courses this time?

Tibby smiles, her fingers hovering over the keyboard. Lila wraps an arm around her shoulder as they walk, one eye briefly peering down at Tibby's phone. Lila releases her, raising a questioning eyebrow. She punches at the phone's keyboard.

Only if you're still buying.

She slides her phone into her coat pocket, passing through the doors that Lila holds open, into Powdered Temptation—lighter and sweeter than ever.

Overnight Cinnamon Rolls

Cinnamon Rolls

Dough Ingredients

- 4 extra large egg yolks
- 1 extra large egg
- ¼ cup white sugar
- 6 tablespoons butter
- ¾ cup buttermilk
- 4 cups flour
- 1 package instant dry yeast
- 1 ¼ teaspoons salt

Filling Ingredients

- 1 cup light brown sugar
- 1 tablespoon ground
- cinnamon
- 1 ½ tablespoons butter

Icing

Ingredients

- ¼ cup cream cheese, softened
- 3 tablespoons milk
- 1 ½ cups powdered sugar

If time allows, let the eggs and buttermilk sit until they reach room temperature. (I never have enough time and always skip this step-- oh well!)

Melt the butter. Whisk together the egg yolks, egg, sugar, butter, and buttermilk in a stand mixer using the whisk attachment. Add 2 cups of flour, yeast and salt.

Switch out the whisk attachment for the dough hook. Add the remaining flour. Knead on low speed for 5 minutes, until the dough clears the sides of the bowl.

Turn the dough onto a lightly floured work surface. Knead by hand, turning it about ten times. Oil a bowl and place the dough in it. Cover and let sit for 2 1/2 hours to rise.

For the filling, mix together the sugar and cinnamon. Melt the butter.

After the dough has risen, turn it onto a floured work surface. Roll the dough into an 18 x 12 inch rectangle, shaping it as you go. Brush the dough with the melted butter. Sprinkle the filling on top, gently pressing in with your hands once completely covered. Beginning with the long edge nearest you, roll the dough into a tight cylinder, placing it seam side down. Cut into 12 rolls. Place in a buttered 9 x 13 glass baking dish. Cover with plastic wrap and let sit overnight.

The next morning, remove the rolls from the refrigerator and let sit on the counter for 30 minutes. Fill a 9 x 13 pan with boiling water. Set the cinnamon rolls on one rack and the boiling water in another rack below it, do not turn on the oven. Let sit for approximately 30 minutes.

Remove the boiling water and the cinnamon rolls. Preheat the oven to 350°. Place the rolls in the middle rack and bake until golden brown, approximately 20 to 25 minutes.

Make the icing. Spread over the rolls when they come out of the oven and serve immediately.

Additional Notes

A Christmas morning essential. Pairs well with strong coffee. Encourages denial, oozes comfort, and effortlessly postpones discussion of last night's gossip.

The End

CUE THE CAROLS. ROLL THE CREDITS.

Want to Stay in Cape Henlopen a Little Longer?

If *Christmas Confessions* was your first visit to Cape Henlopen, there's no need to leave quite yet.

Beach House Confessions is a summer tale that introduces the town and the women whose lives intertwine there. It follows two lifelong best friends—one a Hollywood star caught in a national scandal, the other a widow carrying secrets of her own—reunited for one unforgettable summer at the beach that unravels everything they thought they knew.

As secrets surface and long-buried truths come to light, friendship, love, and second chances collide.

Readers love it for:

- ✔ **Second-chance romance and emotional women's fiction** set in a charming coastal beach town
- ✔ **Perfect for fans of Elin Hilderbrand, Kristy Woodson Harvey, and Susan Mallery**
- ✔ **Four irresistible recipes** inspired by the characters and seaside setting

Many readers start with *Christmas Confessions*—and then return to experience where it all began.

📖 **Start with *Beach House Confessions* here.**

Available on Kindle, Audible & Paperback

One Last Confession...

Christmas may be over, but not every truth has been told. As a thank-you for reading ***Christmas Confessions***, you're invited to download an exclusive bonus scene set *after* the final page.

Once this last confession lands in your inbox, you'll also receive **The Styled Draft: Insider Edition**—where I share behind-the-scenes details, story inspirations, and early news about upcoming books.

You can also find bonus content and series updates at **karagorskibooks.com**.

🎁 **Unwrap that final confession here** →

Thank you for reading—and for spending a dramatic Christmas together at the shore.
Kara Gorski

Here, the next chapter is always waiting.

Made in the USA
Coppell, TX
30 June 2026

83250394R10121